A Wish Made of Glass

A Wish Made of Glass

A SHLEE W ILLIS

To the Prince of Peace, the healer of every broken heart.

Prologue

When I was a child, I danced with the fey folk.

I met with them many times in a glade at the heart of the wood near my home. I can well remember the way my feet spun, my hair a dark cloud swirling round my face. My laughter twined between the notes of their music as if the two belonged together, and I would dance until I was breathless and spent.

A lithe fey girl would take my hand and laugh as I tried to mimic the steps to the dance. A woman strummed her fingers across the strings of her instrument, nodding in time to the music, a small smile upon her lips. A man tapped his feet, standing near the edge of the trees, while he played a rippling tune on his flute.

And each girl and woman wore slippers as delicate as spun sugar, as clear and beautiful as glass. When their feet flew across the ground in an intricate jig, light spilled gently from those slippers like pent-up joy that could no longer be contained.

With my father away at war and my mother ill at home, the fey were my joy. More than that, they were my kin. Their friendship was like a wave washing over me, or like the wind coursing through my hair. Their love for me was both fierce and gentle.

"I've heard that they carry their hearts within their shoes, the fey," Mother told me once, on a day she felt briefly stronger. "Their dreams, their aspirations, their very breath and life."

I gasped with childish fascination. "But why?" We were walking hand in hand across the sunny lawn. "Isn't that dangerous?"

"Oh, yes." Mother winked at me. "Very dangerous, indeed. They must tread carefully. Oh, so carefully! For every step they take, every leap or stumble or turn of a dance, they are treading upon their own hearts."

I was silent some moments, caught up in the idea of such a thing. I could scarcely fathom the fear and courage it would take to live in such a way.

"And the men?" I asked, frowning. "They don't wear glass slippers." I remembered the feet of the young boy who I had danced with only the night before. Truly, I knew his feet well, for my eyes had been sharp upon them to learn the steps of the dance. They had been clad only in supple doeskin boots.

But my mother said, "The men are no different, Izzy. Perhaps their hearts aren't as obvious as the womenfolk's, but they are there nonetheless. Where do *you* think they are?"

I scrunched my face a moment, thinking hard, then my eyes widened. "On the soles of their shoes. That's where the glass is."

Mother pulled me down to sit with her on a bench beneath the willow. "Exactly right," she said. "They tread upon their own hearts as well, even if most can't see it." She gave a weary sigh and closed her eyes. I leaned my head on her shoulder and we sat in silence for some minutes.

"I'm glad we don't have to do that," I said resolutely at last.

"Do what, darling?" Mother's eyes were slow to open, as if she woke from a dream.

"Walk every day upon our own hearts."

"Oh." Mother shifted to look into my face. "Yes. It is a dangerous game, being the possessor of your own heart." With the back of her fingers, she gave my cheek a brief caress. I was shocked to see that her eyes brimmed with wet sadness.

"What is it?" I asked, instantly worried. "Are you missing Father? He'll come home, you know. The war will soon be over."

"I'm well, Isidore," she answered, giving me a tight hug. "Don't fret. I'm well."

Three days later, my mother died.

I was eleven years old. Old enough to see grief baring its teeth at me, but young enough that I could not understand how to protect myself from it. For weeks I stoppered my heart, shelved it and pushed it aside. I refused to visit the fey folk. When I thought of their dancing feet and smiling faces at all it was with a rush of hot anger. Such happiness was only a sham. Such joy must surely be no more than a dream.

Thus my mother's death brought another death in its wake, for my belief in the fey folk died, too. She had been the only one to believe the wild tales I brought home of sun-spackled, laughter-filled frolics in the wood. She had believed in the folk as surely as I had. But something in me was broken now she was gone, and it had been that part of me which had loved the woodland dances and those who danced with me there.

I could not decide how much of the sadness I felt was for my mother's death and how much was mourning for the kin of my heart. The fey.

Weeks passed and at last I ventured to their glade. But it was only to find nothing at all. Not simply an empty place, but a place full of its emptiness, a silent void screaming sorrow in my face. I gazed at the mossy ground where my feet had once been so nimble. Those feet were good for nothing now, save perhaps a funeral march. The trees sighed heartbreak around me as if they too felt the absence of the folk. In truth, the whole forest had grown cold without them.

But then, I told myself, *the fey had never been real.* They had only been a beautiful dream, cruelly taken and crushed beneath my heartbreak. Believing this, I turned to a world which felt bleak as death. I was desolate and alone.

In the end it was Father who coaxed my heart out from hiding.

He came home from the wars once and for good, determined to bring me to life, set upon making me happy. And he did. He gentled my broken heart as if it were a wild animal, he spoke softly to it until it learned to trust him. And like that, he won me.

Though the fey folk left a gaping wound in my heart, and though my mother's death left me hollow and dry, I quickly learned to pour everything into my father and to draw my hope from him. The fey danced from my mind like wisps of fancy, or clouds on the wind. Soon they were gone altogether.

I did not know Father well. He had been away for the better part of my childhood. But now he was here to stay and I did not think to begrudge him a moment of the time we had been apart. Just as he began to make my happiness his chief concern, I too made his happiness my priority.

My mother had been the softer part of me, the whimsy and the dreams and the sweetness of childhood. But those things were gone now, and I was changed. Father led me into the dazzling light of day. I was awake and would dream no more. That is how I wanted it to be. That was the only way I knew how to put aside the sorrow that otherwise might have drowned me.

I was happy thus for nearly three years.

Then my father took a wife.

Chapter One

My knuckles dimple as I gather my full skirts and offer Father a pretty curtsy. I am breathless from running down the stairs to greet him, although, in truth, my breathlessness is mostly from my plumpness, which is the effect of too many sweets these past three years. My old maid Hazel, who has been with me since Mother's death, calls it baby fat, but that is only her love for me speaking. I know better.

But in this moment I do not care one way or another.

"Father." I can barely keep myself from rushing into his arms. He has been gone these past few weeks on business. I am fourteen and am supposed to know nothing of these things, but I have ears and eyes and I know our estate is in dire need of funds.

"Isidore, my love. What are you doing standing there, when you should be here in my arms?" The familiar deep voice booms at me and the white smile flashes beneath his mustache. In another moment, I am embracing him. I feel the warmth of his kiss on my head.

I pull back more quickly than I intend. There is something wrong. I can sense it. "What is it?" I ask, pulling my brows together.

Father laughs. "My, what a face. Nothing is wrong. In fact, everything will be right at last."

My face brightens. "Are our money troubles over, then?" As soon as I see Father's slight frown, I know I should not have said this. Still, I am eager to know the answer.

"I don't know where you got such a notion," Father answers in a clipped voice. "Certainly not from me. No, Izzy, my news is of a different kind entirely, and has nothing at all to do with something as tedious as money." He pulls a face at me and I giggle. Taking my hand, he leads me to a chair near the window.

"You sit, too, Father," I say, but he shakes his head. His heels clack together on the marble floor, something he does only when he is nervous. My heart gives a tiny flutter of fear.

"You are to have a new mother, Iz." Father blurts the words as if he cannot wait to be rid of them. He cannot know they are the same as a knife in my heart.

"But," I manage to gasp, "I have a mother already."

Father turns sharply at the desperate sound of my voice and kneels before me. "Izzy, please," he says. I have never heard such a whine in his voice before. I want to draw back from it. "Please try to understand. I will love no one as I did your mother. This marriage . . . it is necessary, Izzy."

My head is spinning. Necessary? I am young, yes, but when I think of marriage it is accompanied by thoughts of love and respect, even kisses and embraces. Necessity has no place in marriage. Does it?

And this is when I understand.

"You mean she has money." My voice is flat, though tears are hot just behind my eyes. "That's what you're saying, isn't it?"

Father's face tells me all I need to know. His dark eyes swim with a mixture of indignation that I have discovered the truth so quickly, and with sadness that this has come to pass.

He only says, "We will get through this together, Iz, you and I. We will." He gives my hand a squeeze, but I slide it from his grasp. I cannot help it. "My wife is a kind woman, you'll see."

I freeze. "Your wife?"

Father's head is bowed over my hand so I cannot see his face, but his shoulders droop like a man defeated. If the soldiers in his company had ever see him thus just before a battle, they would never have plucked the bravery to march at all.

"Do you mean," I continue, nearly choking on the words, "that you are married already?"

Father's whole body changes as he makes the decision to forego excuses or explanations and simply own up to the truth. I must grant him a begrudging respect for that, at least.

"Yes, I am married, Iz." He rises from his knees. His gaze is direct, though troubled. "If that causes you pain, I am sorry for it from my heart. But . . ." He struggles to find the words and ends by using the same ones he has said to me already. ". . . it was necessary."

But I am far away already. The words he says mean only one thing to me. He has taken back the gift he gave, the only thing that sustained me through this darkness. Himself.

I am not sure I can forgive him for it.

Hazel is sewing by the hearth when I stumble into my bedroom. I am breathing heavily from climbing the three flights of steps to my chamber. I cross in front of the mirror, ignoring the image mimicking my every movement. I know, without looking, what I would see there. A thicker middle, fuller arms, rounder cheeks than any of the other girls I know. I tug angrily at the high collar of my dress and go to stand at the open window where a breeze is blowing.

"What is it, love?" My old nurse's chair scrapes on the floor. In another moment, her bony arms are around my shoulders, her bristled gray hair rough against my cheek.

She clucks and soothes while I tell her everything. And as my story spills out, so at last do the tears.

"Now, now, my darling girl, don't you worry about your father. A man needs a wife and a girl needs a mother. I can't put it simpler than that. It seems to me that your father's marriage fixes both of those problems, doesn't it?"

I turn on her like a ferocious animal. "I don't need another mother."

She is unruffled by my tone and only reaches to smooth the hair which sticks to my tear-stained face. She has known me too long and too well to take my anger amiss.

"No one can take your mother's place. Of course not. How silly of you to even suspect it's possible," she says. "Only remember the fey folk and how they sustained you when you needed them. They'll do it again, I'm certain."

I bridle at her words. It has been a long while since I have given a thought to the fey. "You can't comfort me with fairy stories," I huff, pulling from my nurse's touch.

"Fairy stories! Well, I like that." Hazel snicks her tongue against the roof of her mouth. "Don't dare to tell me you can't remember the fey folk singing in the night, just at the time you missed your mother most?"

A memory wriggles for attention at the edge of my mind, but I quickly shut it out. "I don't remember any such thing," I say as I cross my arms. But my anger has lost its steam and Hazel knows it. She draws me to the bed and makes me sit beside her.

"It was just after I came to your father's household, a night soon after your mother died. Your father was not yet home from the war. You lay on your bed, weary from weeping. I went to draw the curtains, and down on the lawn near the edge of the trees they stood. The fey folk. They sang a lament that would break a heart made of stone. Well, it certainly made these old eyes cry, though they don't often do so easily." She touches one of her withered cheeks as though the ghost of her tears is still there. "The fey prince himself was there leading the rest of them with dark, solemn steps. I could have sworn his eyes were on the window where I stood. I could feel the heat of them, even from such a distance." She glances sideways at me. "O'course you didn't see the folk, lying on your bed as you were. I know you heard them, though, for you grew still as death and your dark eyes were so bright I thought they had turned to burning coals. You didn't move even a finger, yet your whole body changed when you heard their music, as if you had let go of a small piece of your sorrow." Hazel pauses and her hand slides over to cover mine. "You understood they were singing for you, my girl. You knew they heard your broken heart weeping, and that they had come to bring you comfort."

My chest is tight enough to burst. I do not remember this story, but its truth rings through me like a gong and leaves me trembling to my toes.

Hazel nods. It is clear she believes her words have consoled me. "Well, the fey folk will be with you even in the North." She sighs, and her next words are so quiet I think she must be speaking to herself. "They are faithful, even if we are not."

For one wild moment, I ache to believe her. Her words are fire and I am only a fluttering moth. It takes everything in me not to propel myself straight into their warmth.

Perhaps I should visit the glade once more, come sundown. The thought is unbidden, and it makes my heart leap like a hare frightened from its hiding place. Might I see them again, even after these years of silence? I imagine their faces and their bright, smiling eyes. I nearly hear their music which, after all this time, is still mixed in with my blood and marrow.

My shoulders stiffen as I remind myself that I am a child no more, but a girl who has put fairy stories aside and replaced them with graver things. No, I will not visit the glade. I will never visit it again.

Yet that night, in the dark of my room, a memory comes tapping at the door of my mind. Perhaps it is no memory at all, but only an imagining of something that never was. Either way, I do the unthinkable. I let it in.

The fey jig danced that night had been uncommonly swift and complex. I had already talked and laughed and played games the night through. What happened next was inevitable, I suppose. My young feet entangled themselves together trying to find the quick beat of the song, and I tumbled into the brush at the edge of the glade. Dancers eddied around me. None of them had noticed the small human child at their feet. In the chaos of noise and laughter, a hand reached to lift me. Its touch was gentle as mist, but I could never have mistaken the steely strength in it, too.

Angry tears ran down my round cheeks. My knee was bleeding. Worse, so was my pride. I only just had time to glimpse glinting eyes and the curve of a smiling mouth as I was whisked to my feet and tucked beneath the arm of the one who had lifted me. There I stayed until my eyes drooped closed into deep, childish exhaustion. I had awoken in my own bed the next morning, never having seen my rescuer's face.

As soon as this memory floods through me, I know that is just what it is. A memory. A truth. Not an imagined story. The fey folk were there, living in the wood as surely as I am lying in my bed. Now they are gone, just as Mother is gone. Now they are silent, just as my heart is silent.

For all the sorrow these thoughts should bring me, I cannot help but remember the touch of the hand that lifted me and comforted me when I had fallen in the dance, sweet as any father would have done. I hold my own hand up before my face in the dusky light of my room, as if I might be able to discern the mark left there from the fey touch. I clench my fingers into a fist and hold them tight against my heart beneath the covers.

Unaccountably, I feel my lips turn up into a faint smile.

Chapter Two

Father tells me we are to leave the middle country. Our home is to be sold, its ghosts and memories given over to a faceless family who will never care for them. His new wife lives in the North, so it is to the North we must go to begin life anew.

At first I can scarcely stomach it. I thought I was angry before, but now I am snapping and spitting with a fury like consuming fire. One thing alone keeps me from locking myself in my room and refusing to leave my home. It is the thought of my father's wife. At least she will not tread these floors, I think. At least she will not put her hands on my mother's things and haunt the rooms where my mother lived and died. It is this thought alone which gives me any happiness in leaving my home.

Still, even the comfort of this thought hits me with something that feels close to pain.

The next weeks are a flurry of preparations as the servants pack and carry. Though I am only fourteen, I have taken charge of the details of my father's travels many times before. However, this journey is one I cannot keep my heart from rebelling against, and I refuse to take part in organizing it. Father sees and says nothing. He has grown nearly as quiet as I these past days.

At last the final plans are laid and the day of our departure arrives. As our carriage rumbles down the lane, it pleases me to imagine a part of myself, broken off from who I am now, standing on the lawn beneath the sweep of willow branches. I can picture how she is waving goodbye. And though I am leaving her behind, she is yet smiling. For she will stay to haunt the shadows of the empty rooms here and walk the wood and dance in the glade. She will never be troubled by sorrow again. I make a silent, solemn wish that she will one day come and find me.

Hazel holds my hand. Though I want to pull it from her and tell her I am not a child, I refrain. It comes to me that it would be foolish to push away even the tiniest bit of comfort, when I have so little left at all. My gaze is drawn to Father's face. He sits across from us in the carriage, silent and grim. His head is turned as if he is gazing out the window, although instinct tells me his eyes focus only on empty space. He is pale and there are silver strands in the black of his beard I never noticed before. I realize with a jolt that his pain is as great as mine. Perhaps he just has a different way of showing it.

My hand flutters with the impulse to reach out to him, to say a word or offer a touch which might take some of the anguish from his eyes. But then I remember that he has offered me no such word or touch of comfort. Stubbornness flares in me, strengthened by the pain already there. My hand lies quiet on my lap and I close my eyes.

It is a long journey to the North, and it gets colder each mile of the way. Just as I begin to give up hope that we will ever arrive, we do. Father's team of horses pulls our carriage past the square frosty hedges of a sprawling garden. I can see the pointy heads of dwarf evergreens, speckled here and there and tipped with snowy caps. At the end of the long drive, the house regards us like a proud white cat sitting on its haunches. It watches me as though I am the mouse it will devour for supper.

I told my father already, in no uncertain terms, that I cannot call this new woman *Mother*. He was quick to agree, and asked simply that I call her *Stepmother*. I cannot refuse him this small thing. Besides, it will not inconvenience me so very much to call her this, for I plan on calling her nothing at all unless there is no help for it.

As we stamp snow from our shoes in the entrance hall, a woman sweeps down the stairs to greet us. It can be no one but my father's wife, yet I am astonished to see that she is nothing like I imagined. She is hardly taller than I am. Her faded gold hair is piled plainly but elegantly on her head. The figure beneath her tasteful dress is plump and comfortable. In her bright gaze and in the shape of her face I see she was once a beauty. She forgets to offer me a smile in her rush to get to Father's side. It is exactly the thing I have done many times before. When I see her do it, pain lurches in my breast, as if stone is growing around the edges of my heart.

"Stepmother." The curtsy I sweep is over-deep, just bordering on mockery.

"Isidore." She nods, but shows no indication of understanding the irony of my display. Indeed, she is finding it hard to tear her eyes from my father. I must take a slow breath to keep myself from shouting at her to release him.

At last she turns, a slight flush on her face, and says, "And my daughter, your new sister." One of her white hands goes out to indicate a figure who is standing at the edge of the shadows in the corner of the hall. I give a little start. I had not seen her there.

"This is Blessing," my stepmother says, and I hear the whisper of slippered shoes as Blessing steps from the shadows.

I freeze when I see her face. For a moment, I think madly that she must be one of the fey. I have never seen such perfection in anyone's features but theirs. Blessing's smile is shy. Her eyes are like sapphires fixed upon my face. I find I cannot keep myself from smiling back at her.

She is of an age with me, but that is where our similarities end. Where I am lumpiness and childish bulges, Blessing is slender elegance, budding already into delicate womanhood. Where my hair is coarse and dark as a raven's, Blessing's is fine liquid gold streaming over her shoulders.

Her curtsy to me is light as air and, as I return it, I suddenly feel as awkward as the performing bear in the circus Mother and I once visited. But when I look up, Blessing's smile has grown into a grin and her large eyes sparkle. It is a blast of warmth on the chill at my core.

"Well, girls, you run along and get acquainted with one another," Father says. "We shall see you at dinnertime."

I feel a fleeting stab of betrayal that Father would think to leave me like this, awkwardly, with a stranger and in a strange place. And not just any stranger, but someone he insists I call sister. Not just any place, but this cold, vast house he insists is to be my new home.

Blessing's warm hand wriggles into mine. "We could get you unpacked," she says, and my face falls, for I am bored just thinking of it. Then I notice the gleam of mischief in her eyes as she continues, "But I'd much rather show you the hideaways in the house. There are even one or two Mother doesn't know about."

I am unwilling to smile, yet somehow there is one slipping onto my lips. I am unwilling to accept so swiftly what I have raged against for weeks, yet I am nodding before I can stop myself.

"Hideaways?" I say. "Truly?"

Blessing's golden curls bob as her head moves up and down. "Of course! This fusty old house has plenty. I've lived here my whole life and have had lots of time to find them. You must promise not to tell anyone when I show you. Swear?"

"Yes!" I breathe. I am utterly drawn in. The worry of these past days falls from my shoulders. Even the lingering sadness from Mother's death is not so sharp in this moment. I am once again a child, ready to play childish games.

"There is time to show you one before dinner," Blessing says, tugging me along up the stairs. "It's behind the attic stairwell. We must wait to see the other hiding places, but there will be plenty of time later."

I follow her willingly. I do not even look over my shoulder to glance at the resentment I leave behind me like a cast-off rag.

By all rights I should hate her, this beautiful creature who is everything I am not, who is everything I should be. Yet a cord has been woven between us at this crucial moment, in these fragile seconds. Cords like this one often prove strongest.

Just like that, we are sisters.

Father and his new wife leave on their wedding journey three days later. They tell us they will be gone two months. Again I feel the sting of betrayal. I wonder that Father is marrying this woman of necessity, yet spending two months of pleasure far from me. Has he not told me many times I am the one who holds his heart? I begin to doubt I have ever had it at all. I begin to wonder if the closeness I felt between us these years was merely a cruel mirage.

Yet Blessing is with me in the swirl of snow on the wide front stairs as we bid our parents farewell. And when I see the pain in her face as the carriage disappears from sight, I tuck her arm against mine with a squeeze. My father has left me alone here on the verge of this new and strange life. Her mother has done the same.

It is another cord woven between us.

Chapter Three

The North is cursed cold, I soon learn. Yet a frosty garden proves a perfect place for young girls to amuse themselves. We run along the stony, twisting paths and through a maze of hedges in a game of chase and find. When we tire of that, we sit on the icy iron bench nestled beneath the branches of a fir tree and do our secret-telling.

The whispered confidences of two girls of fourteen are doubtless laughable to most. But Blessing and I know they are sacred. We know they are merely a way of promising, a swearing of our newly found sisterhood. Boys spit on their palms or cut their fingers and let the blood run together. Girls tell secrets. So we tell ours, and before a week is gone there is almost no corner of my heart Blessing has not seen. She is my sister now, in truth.

When Father has been gone a month, the trees begin showing tiny green and pink buds. By the time he returns, the whole countryside will be awash with spring. It will come a full month later than our springtime in the middle country, true, but the North is almost a world of its own. It wears its frost as a queen of snow might wear her royal cloak, proud and white. The North is so different, in fact, I catch myself wondering if the fey folk are here as Hazel claimed they would be. The prick of homesickness, sharp and thin as a needle, reaches my heart at the thought of that. Not merely a longing for my homeland and the house of my childhood, but a longing for the folk themselves, the fey who used to love me so.

At least, I imagined they loved me, before I knew it was all pretend.

One day, as Blessing and I approach the farthest side of the garden, I stop. "What's beyond these bushes?" I ask, hopping awkwardly on tip-toe to see over the tall hedge.

"Only the forest." Blessing's voice is dismissive.

"How can you say only the forest?" I ask, aghast. "No forest is *only* a forest."

The memory comes of fey feet dancing, quick as light and shadow on the mossy forest floor. I try to push it away, but it is too late. My heart is fluttering against my ribs and I know nothing will stop me from getting a glimpse of this forest Blessing dismisses so easily.

"Izzy, what in the world are you doing?" Blessing watches with wide eyes as I grunt and heave, pushing the hedges apart to make a path between them. It is no small feat for a girl like me who is more accustomed to books and chocolate than to vigorous activity such as this. In less than two minutes there is dampness beneath my arms and beading on my forehead.

"Help me, Blessing," I say irritably. Just as I think I must be close to working my way out the other side, a hand grasps my shoulder. Blessing yanks me away from the hedge with a strength I never would have credited.

I open my mouth to say something sharp to her, but fall silent when I see how white her face is, and how large her blue eyes in it. "It's forbidden," she whispers. "I am forbidden to go there and so are you. What did you think you were doing, Iz?"

I gape at her a moment and then do the only thing I can think of. I laugh. "What do you mean, forbidden? Who says so? Why?"

"Mother has always said so, since I was a child." Blessing casts a glance at the ragged hole I have worked in the hedge. "Once you've lived in the North long enough, you'll understand."

Now I am well and truly exasperated. "So there are monsters in the forest, is that what you're trying to say?"

"No." Blessing's chin lifts a little. She is offended I would accuse her of believing in monsters. Very well, then.

"Well, I won't know until someone tells me," I remind her none too gently. "But," I shrug, "if you are too frightened to speak of it . . ."

Before I can take full advantage of my own bluff by turning from her, Blessing blurts, "It is the fey."

My heart begins to thunder so loud it will be a miracle if anyone in the North does not hear it.

"What?" I manage to croak at last. I work hard to control my face, though I fear it is of little use. I nearly spill everything then. I nearly hand Blessing this one last secret, the only one I have kept from her. That I have known the fey. Danced with them, sang with them, touched their hands.

But I do not tell it. I do not speak. Somehow I cannot. My mouth will not cooperate. My throat contracts in rebellion. If I am honest, I know it is because this secret is my most precious. I am not sure if I could hand it so easily to anyone. Even Blessing.

So I say, hating myself for uttering the words, "Stories? Wives tales, do you mean, about fairies and such? Surely you don't believe in those things, Blessing."

Blessing's hair bounces on her shoulders as she shakes her head. "I thought they were," she says. "All my life I thought they were simply stories told to keep children from wandering too far. Until . . ." Her expression changes. One moment it is fearful and the next it is full of a strange but undeniable calm. That is when I know for certain she has seen the fey for herself.

"When did you see them?" I cut quickly to the core of it. Jealousy rages beneath my skin, screams in each beat of my heart. The fey were mine. Are mine. Now I face the thought that perhaps

I am no more special than anyone else who happens to wander into their wood.

Blessing's mouth turns up in a guileless smile and she takes my hand. I walk beside her like a wooden toy, staring straight ahead as we make our way to the house.

"It was just once," she says. "It was the very day you arrived, Izzy. In the morning, when I was sick with worry at your arrival, I looked out my window." She sighs, remembering. "There they were, a half a dozen of them, straight and strong beneath their cloaks. I nearly missed them, for the mist was thick all around the edge of the wood. But somehow I think they wanted to be seen. They wished me to see them, so I would know everything would be fine."

It takes me a moment to understand. Then it is all I can do not to whoop with joy right there on the front steps of the house. As it is, I am nearly drowning in happiness.

They came for me. They followed me. They are here in this frozen land, far from their home, because of their love for me.

The disbelief I clung to these past three years falls away like chaff. I am amazed it took me so long to see through its flimsy mask.

They came on the day I arrived. They came for me, my shameless heart sings.

I grin at Blessing. I cannot help it. She grins back. The wind ruffles the fur on our hooded cloaks, so sweet it is as if spring herself has reached down to kiss us.

"Do you believe me?" she asks, drawing her brows together in a charming show of worry.

"Yes, I do." I lean to give her a swift kiss on the cheek. This new knowledge has burned away the bile of jealousy I felt moments before. "I will always believe you, no matter what."

Chapter Four

The deepest hour of the night has come, the hour the night birds and the insects revere with their silence. I cannot think what woke me. Stillness ripples like silk all around my chamber. Yet something is different. The air is thick with an unspoken, undeniable promise.

I go still at the touch of something on my hair. It is a caress, delicate as a moonbeam. This night is so strange, anything may be possible. That is the only way I can account for the feeling that rises in me, half anguish and half elation. As I twist around beneath the covers, the word slips from my mouth before I can call it back.

"Mother."

But the face I look into is not my mother's. It is the face of a young woman, beautiful and lithe as a willow. I know at once she is one of the fey folk. The tips of her ears curve into gentle points beneath the swoop of her hair. Shadows move across her features, and it is hard to tell, but I think she is familiar to me. She looks to be not many years older than I, though the fey do not age as humans do. She might be a century old or more for all I know.

As I shift to sit up, she clicks her tongue against her teeth. "No, no," she says. "Lie still. I'm nearly finished."

Obediently, I stop moving. All but my head, which I turn slowly to see what she is doing. Her long fingers are working my hair into a series of looping, intricate braids. I give a little gasp when I see that each twist of the braid is interlaced with dozens of tiny flowers. They are Northern flowers. I have seen them over the garden hedge, scattered at the edge of the forest. Blessing told me they are called Dewdrops. The fair, watery blue of them is a striking contrast with the black of my hair.

"There!" The fey girl says with a satisfied breath. A smile flits to her mouth and is gone in the space of a moment. "Finished."

"It's lovely," I whisper, although my gaze is still fastened on her face. "Thank you."

I am not sure what to do or what to say. I am almost afraid to move at all for fear this is a dream and it will disperse like fog if I dare to breathe on it. Yet the fey girl's hand is real enough as she rests it coolly on my arm.

"Isidore," she says softly. I wait to see if she will say more, but she allows silence to unravel between us.

Her hair is the color of rich earth and her eyes are as green as forest ferns. They are the eyes of a friend, I am sure. The night is so still and her presence is so comforting that I begin to grow drowsy. It is just as my eyes begin to flutter closed that I remember how I know her. She used to play the fiddle as I danced in the fey glade, her bare feet tapping the rhythm upon the moss between the bright, speckled toadstools.

I open my mouth to whisper this memory to her, but she is speaking already.

"Be strong, Isidore," she says, squeezing my hand as if she would transfer strength straight to my veins. Over her shoulder, from within the deeper shadows of my room, I think I see the glint of midnight eyes. I lift up on one elbow, straining to see the face to whom they belong. But her voice is a lullaby I cannot resist, and I am suddenly weary to my bones.

I am falling fast, yet not so fast that I do not hear the last thing she says. Her voice becomes as rich as the deepening night. "Dear one, do not lose your heart."

When I wake the next morning my belly is wound in sorrowful knots, for I do not doubt I have dreamed every second of the
fey woman's visit. The folk have not shown themselves to me in
years. Why would they do so now?

Yet when I rise, I find the delicate blue petals of Dewdrops
strewn across my pillow. And when I leap from my bed to twist
before the mirror, I see tiny flowers woven through my braids, as
bright as winking stars against a night sky.

My joy at knowing the fey are near is full to bursting over the next
few days. Both Hazel and Blessing see the change in me, although
they attribute it to the fact that Father will return soon.

As if Blessing's account of the fey folk on the day of my arrival
had not been enough to thrill my blood, now I have seen them
with my own eyes. It is as if I have believed someone I loved was
dead, only to discover they have been alive and waiting for me
years on end. If only I had been able to open my eyes and see it
before now.

I determine then and there that I will forget the hurt Father
has caused and throw myself into his arms when he returns home,
just as I used to do. I will even embrace my stepmother and kiss
her hands and learn to know her better. Indeed, I believe I am
ready to love anyone at all.

When Father and his wife return from their journey a week
later, Blessing and I are ready for them. Hazel has washed and
brushed our hair until it gleams, and scrubbed our faces pink. For
a reason baffling to me, she thought it would bring our parents
pleasure to see us dressed alike, thus she commissioned matching
dresses. It is unfortunate for me that I am fully twice Blessing's
width, which is exaggerated by the ridiculous frills on our frocks.
However, even this cannot stem my excitement.

Nothing can go wrong. Not now. Not in this moment.

With our noses pressed to the chill windowpane, Blessing and I watch as our parents alight from the carriage. From Father's quick, white smile as he shares a joke with the driver, I see immediately that he is in high spirits. My heart flips with anticipation.

In another moment, he is in the hall coming toward us, his wife floating on his arm. He brings the smell of cool spring air with him, of green and growing things. His smile spreads wider beneath his mustache when he sees us. I return it, ready to spring into his arms the instant he opens them to me.

"My daughters." His voice rings through the hall like a deep bell. "How I've missed you. Come give your father a hug."

Blessing releases her hold on my hand and surges forward. Her laugh tinkles like music next to his booming one as she wraps her arms around his neck.

But I stand still as death, my belly churning a sickening hot and cold. The word that Father has so carelessly uttered is beating at my heart like a hammer.

Daughters.

"Izzy, you've not missed me, then?" Father calls, holding out the arm not wound around Blessing. "Your sister is quick to greet me, as you see. Are you unwell?"

"But—" My words stumble out before I can stop them. "But, Father, Blessing is not your daughter. I am."

Silence descends on the hall as if I have spoken the words to a curse. I hear the quiet swish of silk as my stepmother puts her hand to her mouth in a dainty show of shock. Blessing's knuckles whiten as she grips Father's shoulder, and I must look away from the pain on her face. Father's smile is gone, but when he speaks, his voice is gentle.

"Isidore, that's no way to talk, you know. Blessing is your sister now that her mother and I are wed. Of course, that means she is my daughter as well."

"I am your only daughter." My voice grows steadier as a flicker of fury begins to burn in my chest.

Father gives me a hard look. I immediately read his thoughts on his face. I do not love him so well for nothing. His eyes say, *Of course you are my only daughter, though this is neither the time nor place for such an argument.*

I recognize what he is doing for Blessing. He did it once for me. He knows as well as I that we are a patchwork family at best, with this marriage of necessity. But he is determined to make Blessing love him, as he was once determined to win my heart. It is in his nature to make people feel cherished. It is one of the reasons I love him as I do. Can I fault him for something so true and good?

Yet I see him kneeling there, one arm wrapped around Blessing, his wife standing at his side, and it is as if I am looking at a portrait. A portrait of which I am no part. It cuts me to the quick and I can feel my heart begin to bleed.

"Izzy, may we speak of this later?" Father asks quietly. "Perhaps I will come to your room."

"No," I say so abruptly I startle myself. "What is there to speak of? You have two daughters now, that's all."

But I have loved Blessing, I want to tell him. I called her sister and, more than that, I took her into my very heart as a true sister. I barely understand it myself. Even with the love I have for Blessing, I cannot stand the thought of Father calling her *daughter*. It is the same fierce possessiveness I felt when Blessing spoke of seeing the fey folk. There is no explaining it. I simply know it is gripping me by the throat so tightly I can scarcely draw breath.

"Anthony." My stepmother's voice is a breathy whisper. "I don't want to cause any–"

Father holds up a hand and gets to his feet. "It's not your fault." His voice is suddenly weary. "I would like to rest in the library a while before dinner," he says. "Izzy, will you come?"

I long to say yes. I ache to say it, and to follow him, and to make everything as it should be. But he is no longer mine. Even now, my stepmother is taking hold of his arm and drawing him away. She will not leave his side, not even to let me greet him properly. Jealousy and hurt are gnawing at me like a dog worrying at a bone. Though they are a misery, I am quick to recognize them as my one defense. So I cling to them and shake my head. Angry, hopeless tears stab at the back of my eyes.

"I'm going to my room," I say with stiff politeness. "I will see you at dinner, Father. Welcome home, Stepmother."

My stepmother eyes me as if I am a wild animal that will snap at her as sure as speak to her. Then she nods and offers a nervous smile. Father sighs and takes her arm as they make their way from the hall.

"Blessing," I say, turning to my sister. She is the one bright spot remaining in this accursed day. "Will you come upstairs and help me out of this dress before Hazel can stop me?" I give a halfhearted laugh. "I've not ever hated a dress as much as I hate this one."

But I am shocked to see Blessing's lovely face flushed with an emotion I have never seen in her before now. Anger.

"Why would you not say I'm your sister?" Her voice wobbles.

Though I should have foreseen this, I am still taken aback by her question. I stutter, "Blessing, I . . . I thought you'd understand. Of course you're my sister! Haven't I said as much, many times?"

"Then what is wrong?" she demands, one hand on her slender hip.

"Father didn't ask me to call you sister, did he? *He* called you *daughter.*" My voice goes flat. "You aren't his daughter."

"No." Her brows arch. "No more than you are my sister."

I can say nothing to that. Her words are true, of course, but they only prove she does not understand in the least. I do not understand it myself, truly. I can only repeat, sounding dull-witted, "You aren't his daughter."

The rift between us is tearing open, wider every moment. I can almost hear it, like rich fabric splitting asunder. If it were in my power to reach out and stop it, I would. But I do not know how.

Blessing watches me a few more moments, then gives a huffing, angry sigh from her nose and turns in a whirl of skirts. Before she leaves, she shoots a withering glance over her shoulder.

"I am going to speak to Father and Mother, even if you won't. It seems to me you're no worthy daughter, behaving this way when they have just arrived home again."

Her anger follows her like a storm cloud down the corridor. When she is gone, her words are still ringing in my ears. She is right. I am honest enough to admit that. I am not a worthy daughter. I have only to look in the mirror to see it.

My former stubbornness and anger dissipate into nothing, and in their place comes a horrid, black emptiness which yawns before me. I fear if I take a step forward I will be swallowed by it. So I do not succumb. I force back the blaze of tears and clench my hands together to stop their trembling. I float to my room like a wraith, barely aware my feet are moving.

A horrible thought slinks into my mind. The fey woman who visited me last night spoke words, and I think now they must certainly have been a warning. She knew, somehow, what was to come. Her words resound in me, clanging against my ribs like cymbals. *Do not lose your heart.*

How? I want to cry like a petulant child. *How can I lose my heart when no one wants it?*

I do not know how much time passes. It is dark beyond the panes of my window when Hazel finds me. She clucks over the wrinkles I have put in my dress by lying on my bed like a heap of rags, and she bids me to rise and eat, since I was rude enough to miss supper.

I do as she tells me, all the while feeling the empty space just below my ribs where my heart used to be. Can Hazel see it in my face? The loss of both father and sister in the space of a day. For that is what this feels like to me. I fear it has turned me into no more than a husk, no better than an aged person who must use a cane with every step she takes.

I wait the evening through to hear a knock on my door. For Father's voice, or Blessing's, on the other side, soft with apology or even sorrow for what they have done to me. What they have made of me. Each minute that I do not hear it, I grow more and more like stone and, at last, when the clock down the hall strikes midnight, I go to bed.

My dreams are disturbed, but when morning comes I am sorry to leave them behind, for waking is much worse.

Chapter Five

Months twist slowly by and turn into years. I grow accustomed to what my life has become. We all do, for we must. Hazel tells me I am turning into a fine young lady, but I know she refers only to my figure, which grows gradually slimmer and taller. As for the rest of me, the part you cannot see, I know her dear old heart frets for it. She has not been my nurse all this time for nothing, and she is not blind to the changes of my heart, even if I do not speak them aloud.

It appears the only patch now in this patchwork family is me. When we sit in the parlor, as we do many nights, I see Blessing's eyes on Father's face, and understanding trickles down my spine. She has never known a father. How could she resist such a man as he, when he opened his arms and heart to her so willingly? He did the same for me when Mother died, and I never dreamed of fighting it. Can I blame Blessing for doing the same, when I can see in her face how hungry she is for his love?

Even so, I cannot see them together or hear them share a joke without thinking how they both betrayed me. Father chose a second daughter and has shamed me by it. Blessing placed his love before mine.

It is a simple thing. I wonder that they cannot see it for what it is. Yet somehow I am given the blame. Somehow it is my words which ring bitter and whose face turns sour as the weeks and months go by.

Three years it continues thus. My decision to distance myself is never made consciously. All the same, that is just what I do. It comes to pass so slowly even I can scarcely see it happening. I ride and sing and recite and learn lessons alongside Blessing. But never do we return to the sisterhood of those first two months. Then, it was the two of us alone with nothing between us except the truth of what we felt. Now, we are commanded to be sisters, and it has poisoned the bloom of friendship that had begun to spring up on its own.

It is the same with Father. I still cling to him in many ways, yet a wedge has been driven between us. Perhaps I am the one who drove it. Day by day it forces us farther apart. His love for me does not dim, and this is perhaps the hardest thing of all. I see it shining from his dark eyes when he speaks to me, and I see the disappointment each time he wishes to spend time with me and is met with rebuff. I cannot forgive him, not fully. I cannot forget. And though life continues normally on the outside, I know Father sees the shadows between us as clearly as I do. I ask myself why he does not simply reach out and sweep them aside. If he loved me, surely he would. I do not think, until it is too late, that each time he looks at me, he may be trying to do that very thing.

Most would think me callous to behave in such a way. I even begin to believe perhaps I have no heart at all. I dismiss this idea quickly, however. For each time I am silent in the face of Father's love, I hear another piece of my heart shatter.

Thus I tell myself there is one thing a broken heart is good for, at least, even if it is only to prove I possess a heart at all.

I begin to wander in the wood.

At first I venture there from sheer obstinacy. I know full well Stepmother has forbidden it. I know, too, that Blessing fears the forest, which is another point in its favor. Yet I am no longer a child of fourteen, but a woman grown, with seventeen years behind me. I do not fear my stepmother's wrath. If I am truthful, she has mostly sweetness in her nature. More so, I do not care for Blessing's fears. I ceased to care for them long ago.

This forest is far different from the woods in the middle country. The trees here are not like the squat, woven-trunked, whispering things I danced amongst as a child. The trees in this wood are straight and proud and tall. They wear their leaves like a gathering of giant kings donning their crowns. The ground here is not covered in a soft carpet of moss and fern, as I am used to, for it is too hard and cold in the North for that. Though the forest floor stretches barren and brown and empty between the great trunks of the trees, there is yet life somewhere far beneath it, wending and pushing below the surface of the earth. It pulses beneath my feet like a promise sleeping in the frozen ground.

I do not wander the wood searching for the fey folk. At least, this is what I tell myself. Since the fey girl visited my room in the dark of night those years ago, I have not glimpsed a hint of the folk. Perhaps they disapprove of me and the changes these years have wrought in my heart. I can account for it no other way. So I seek simply the comfort of the trees and their soft nods and sighs of understanding. They never judge my thoughts. They never name me heartless.

Yet one night, though I do not seek them, I find the fey folk just the same.

The stars have just begun to poke their shimmering holes into the fabric of the black night sky, and the moon is so low I want to reach out and dip my finger in the creaminess of its face. A familiar clearing appears ahead of me. As I approach it, I find it is not empty. Voices drift through the night, as soft as the growth of trees. I can see the faint glow of blue fire bobbing sideways. Fey lanterns.

I crouch low and steal forward. Peering from behind the wide trunk of a tree, I see them. I draw a slow, deliberate breath to keep myself from gasping with pain as homesickness pierces me straight through.

Their familiar figures, tall and cloaked and still, stand in a circle. Though their faces are hidden beneath the deep shadows of their hoods, I feel sure I would know them if I could but see them. Each holds a lantern which flames sapphire light. Beneath the folds of their cloaks peek the blues and greens of the women's dresses and the earthy browns and blacks of the men's shirts. My gaze slides downward and I lift a hand to cover my mouth. For there are the glass slippers, the fey slippers. Silver moonlight catches at them and sends piercing light into my face.

These slippers are the most beautiful things I have yet seen. They are pieces of my childhood, tangible and sparkling. My heart lurches in my chest, as if making a wild attempt at escape. It aches for those slippers. In their lustrous surface I see the happiest moments of my life.

I've heard they carry their hearts within their shoes, the fey.

The memory of my mother's words swings my thoughts into sharp focus. A shiver tiptoes across my shoulders. The fey tread upon their own hearts. Their steps are careful and true. But would mine be, if I were to have a pair of my own slippers?

The last of the folk disappear into the shadows. I am up in an instant and running, practically tripping over my own feet as I fly homeward. When I reach my bedroom, I am breathless and damp with a sheen of sweat. Hazel shuffles to greet me, her wrinkled eyes open wide.

"What's this, my dear? Whatever is the matter?"

Before I can open my mouth to speak, Hazel takes a step back to scrutinize my face. "Oh," she says.

"What?"

"You've seen them, then." She nods once. "You've seen the fey folk tonight."

"How did you know?"

With a gruff laugh, she shakes her grizzled head. "I haven't cared for you all these years for naught, my dear. Come, let me draw your bath and you can tell me about it."

But I cannot wait. My words spill out. "I want to know about them," I say. "Do they grant wishes, as some stories say? Where do they live out there in the forest? In houses like ours?"

For all that I danced and laughed with these folk in times past, for all that they were dear to my heart, I find I know next to nothing of them.

The questions are barely out of my mouth when one of Hazel's bony hands shoots out to grip my jaw. She pushes her face into mine and squints. Skin bunches around her eyes. I am sure I have put some of those wrinkles there myself.

"Why do you want to know?"

"Well, because . . ." I waver. "I suppose because I'm curious. There's nothing wrong with being curious, is there?"

She releases me with a sigh. Her face does not give much away. It never does. But even I cannot miss the fleeting sadness that crosses it now. "No, my darling. Nothing at all. Come, take a bath and eat. I will tell you about them when you are ready for sleep."

I know from experience it is no good arguing with her. I slip from my gown and into the water she has prepared, squealing as it scalds my skin. I submit to her scrubbing, although in my opinion it takes an uncommonly long time. When Hazel brings my supper, I eat it so quickly I nearly choke once or twice and she scolds me roundly. Yet I am in bed a full hour before my usual time, and it is worth it. My nurse settles into her chair and I can see from the expression on her face that she will make good on her promise.

"Now," Hazel says as I flop to get comfortable beneath the covers. "Where shall I begin?"

"I want to know if they grant wishes," I say without hesitation.

Hazel is silent so long I turn to see if she has fallen asleep in her chair, as she sometimes does. But she is staring out the window, a strange look on her worn old face.

"They do grant wishes," she answers at last. "One wish, it so happens. It must be claimed when a winter's full moon shines down on the snow. On such a night, you must find one of the fey folk and grab hold of his hand before he vanishes. Then you must keep hold of it until he agrees to grant your wish."

"Oh," I sigh, sinking into my pillow. A curious smile plays at the corner of my mouth.

Hazel looks at me, her lips set in a grim line. "Even wishes are not always what we think they will be, Isidore. Even wishes may come with a price."

I am quick to shrug off the twinge of discomfort her warning brings. Instead, I am ready with my next question. "Where do they live?"

Hazel favors me a reproachful smile. "Why, in the forest, love, as you well know."

"Yes, but where in the forest?"

I know this part of the story, of course, but it has been long since I have heard it told and I ache to hear it again.

Hazel lays her finely wrinkled hand on top of mine. When she speaks, her voice is scarcely more than a whisper. "Their realm exists in a place between the shadows and the rays of the sun. Their kingdom is woven 'round the trees, with invisible castles towering to the sky, piercing the clouds, unseen pathways winding outward. The entrance to their world is somewhere . . . everywhere. You never know when you may step over the threshold. It is unseen and unheard by most, for most are too busy to see or hear it. Most have not the heart to feel its very nearness. And though the fey realm lies alongside ours, it is as different from our world as the sun is from the moon."

I am trembling as if my skin is not enough to hold me in and my excitement may break free at any moment. Thoughts tumble in my head as Hazel tucks the covers under my chin and her cool lips come down to kiss my forehead.

"One wish?" I ask as she snuffs the candles.

"Yes, my dear, only one. Or so the stories say." A brief slash of grief is in her eyes again as she gazes at me. But I barely notice it.

The moment she is gone, I throw the covers over my head. Thoughts descend on me, clamoring for my attention. I do not know if my mother's words were true. I do not know if the fey truly tread upon their own hearts. But when I looked at the slippers, I saw all that I have lost and more. I saw . . .

I try to force down the wild hope that rises in me, yet it comes anyway.

When I gazed at the fey slippers, I saw my own heart restored.

On the tail of this thought comes the surety that I must have a pair of those slippers for my own. I could not say what propels me into this madness, for even I must admit it certainly feels like madness. Perhaps it is this pining in me that has never yet been satisfied. Perhaps these slippers are the remedy at last.

My heart flutters like a bird in the cage of my breastbone. Thoughts reel through my head. It will be four months at least before snow can be expected. And of course that snow will need to fall on the night of a full moon. And on that night I will need fortune with me for a certainty if I am to find and hold the hand of one of the folk and have my wish granted.

Oh, it will be difficult. I do not try to convince myself otherwise. The chance of my winning this wish will be slight.

If I should win it, though . . .

The thought of having a pair of those slippers for myself should, by all rights, keep me up the night through. Instead it lulls me to sleep, gentle as a mother's lullaby. It is as if this plan I have hatched, this dream I have birthed, is the fulfillment of my hope, an ending to my painful search for happiness. I sink into dreamless slumber, as blissful and deep as the sleep of a newborn child.

Chapter Six

The next day I am deep in a book, sitting beneath the sweeping shade of the garden oak, when a servant comes to find me. Birds warble softly in the branches above as I watch him make his way across the lawn. He jostles along at a quick pace on legs as spindly as a scarecrow's. It is a droll sight and I duck my head to hide my grin while he approaches.

When I am composed enough to look up, he is standing before me and panting like a bellows, a deathly pallor on his face. Observing him in such a state gives me a slight shock, but it is the torment in his eyes that freezes the blood in my veins.

"Joseph?" My book drops to the grass as I jump to my feet. Fear leaps in my belly. "What has happened? Is it Blessing?" I am instantly irked at the swift turn of my thoughts, but Joseph shakes his head.

"No, miss, it's not your sister." He puts a hand to his chest, attempting to catch his breath.

If it is not Blessing, it must be Hazel, I think, for my father and his wife are away from home today.

"What then?" I prod.

"It's your parents," Joseph begins, but makes it no further before his face crumples. He tries so hard to mask his tears and is so unsuccessful at it that I nearly laugh aloud. Nearly. Until I understand what he has just said.

My heart is already drumming like a death knell in my ears. I think it understands before the rest of me does. "They are dead." My whisper is only a ghost of sound. "He—"

He is dead, my heart finishes as what was left of it splinters into infinite pieces.

Joseph nods, confirming my words, tears streaking his cheeks. I want to snatch out my hand and strike the sorrow off his face. How does he dare to cry those worthless tears when I am standing here as dry as an empty well?

The world tilts and sways as if I am a marionette bouncing on a string and my whole life is nothing more than a display, the mere backdrop for the forgery of the days I have wasted thus far. I think everything I have lived until now must have been only make-believe, and that this moment is the harsh, beautiful, undeniable truth.

The truth is that I loved him. The truth is that I forgave him long ago.

But the realization has come too late. It is a knife twisting in me.

"How?" I manage after an eternity has passed. My voice is as rusty as an old woman's.

Joseph swallows and straightens his shoulders a bit, as if remembering to whom he speaks. "The carriage overturned some miles away, miss. Your father lived long enough to send for you. The messenger is still at the house, but—but he says there's no purpose in your going. It was bad, and . . . and by now your father will be—"

Dead. Each time I think the word, sorrow gushes from my heart like blood pulsing from a fatal wound.

"But *how?*" I persist gruesomely, hardly knowing what I say. "Were they thrown from the carriage? Did they break every bone in their bodies? Were they crushed beneath the wheels, or trampled by the horses? How, Joseph? *How?*"

I am shouting, and the poor man gawks at me as if he has seen a ghost. Perhaps this is the very thing he sees, after all. How can I tell? I am certainly not myself. The wetness of tears is on my face, but I cannot think how they could be mine. I can hear a horrible rasping sound, a desolate weeping, but it cannot be me. I thought my heart too destroyed to weep. But now I think its very brokenness may cause me to weep the rest of my life.

In the hall, I speak with the messenger. I cannot bring myself to demand the details of my father's death, as I asked Joseph. He gives a brief, stuttering account as I stare at the shining top button of his coat. The bodies will be carried to the house. The physician has already been sent for. I nearly give a mad burst of laughter when he tells me this.

"You may tell the physician to go tend to the living." Bile rises sharp in my throat. "We don't want him here."

Blessing and Hazel are nearby, weeping softly. I ignore them. Neither of them knows the truth, as I do. Neither of them understands. When the messenger leaves and the hall is silent, I turn on my heel away from them both.

"Izzy." My sister's voice is a raw wound.

It barely reaches me. I have already gathered my loneliness about me like a talisman. I have called out my anger like an army to protect me. I hold my heart close, pressing the broken pieces together in a frantic attempt to salvage them. Speaking, weeping, sharing this grief with her in this moment may destroy me. Blessing must see that I will not come to her because her lovely face distorts with tears and turns ugly for the first time since I have known her.

She does not know. She does not understand. How can she? She was not the daughter who broke his heart. She was not his daughter at all.

A strange hollowness grips me in the following days. I pray it will relinquish its iron hold when Father and his wife are laid to rest. Yet after their bodies have been buried and prayed for and wept over, the emptiness is still there. I think it has come to stay. It has already chiseled out a corner of my heart for its nest, seeped into my bones to mix with the marrow.

Hazel sings to me most nights and tells me all the old stories as my eyes stare at nothing. I know it is her way of pleading with me, of coaxing me from this shell she believes I am trapped within. What she cannot know is that I am helpless to come out of it. I would scream and rant if I thought it would help. But nothing can be the same now, and I cannot forget it was I who made it so. I begin to see Father's face in my dreams, his dark eyes full of pleading sorrow. I remember, too, how I turned away from him time and again.

Days turn to weeks. One night Hazel alights at last upon a tale which spreads light into a small corner of my mourning. It is a tale of the fey folk and, as she tells it, my old nurse's voice is as soft as the moonlight that streams across my pillow.

"There was once a young fey boy who loved a human girl," it starts, and I begin already to sink into the warmth of this story. I let this one word, *loved*, spread its smooth balm through me as I have allowed nothing else to do for so long.

Hazel's voice drones on and my eyelids begin to grow heavy as the tale comes to an end.

"She went to live with him in his country, in the fairy realm itself. She gave up everything for him, and when she arrived at her new home it was to discover he was none other than the fey prince himself. His royal cloak was made of fireflies, his crown woven with sunbeams. Though he was glorious, the girl knew she would not have cared if he had been the humblest of servants in the fey kingdom. Her love for him burned bright and forever. It made her the perfect princess of the fey, and they ruled together for age upon age."

I hear the words of the story, but they are mere sound washing against my ears, for sleep holds me in his arms already. I give up the fight and allow his sweet, dark hands to pull me down.

Chapter Seven

*A*utumn is so slow to seep into the North country that I do not notice summer leaving until it is gone altogether. I am not sorry to see it go. It held only heartache for me.

I return to the wood, the only place I have ever felt truly at home in this land. My feet find the hidden pathways day after day, and each step I take puts a tiny piece of my heart back into place. Rich colors sing all around. The forest's cloak is flushed with crimson and gold and green. I cannot help but reach out and touch it.

I run my hand along a low-hanging branch as I pass beneath its sweep. The leaf I pluck is whorled with color. Its surface is smooth beneath my fingertips. My lips curve upward. It is the first time I have smiled in an age.

Sadness chases it from my face in the next instant.

The sun sinks beneath the rim of the world, and the forest is hungry to soak in the last of its rosy glow. I grow still in these brief moments of in-between, and clasp my hands in something nearing reverence.

"Nothing dies as beautifully as autumn," I breathe, arching my neck to gaze upward.

The leaves on every branch shiver as if acknowledging my words, then give up the last of their colors to the descending night.

Sunlight snuffs out like a candle and in mere seconds I am left in the dark. I had forgotten this is the night of the new moon.

I close my eyes on the panic that rushes upon me, giving myself a moment to think. The house is west of the wood. At least, I think it is. And the sun has just set at my back. That is, if I have not turned slightly since then. I should not have ventured so far, so late. I square my shoulders, prepared to choose a direction and take my chances.

When I turn, my outstretched fingers meet solid warmth. It is the touch of another's hand.

I give a little scream and jump back. The sapphire glow of a lantern makes a hazy sphere of light on the ground. A fey man is standing within it. He is beautiful as a forest night, and his dark gaze and sad smile are as warm as breath across my skin. For a single moment I think I have seen those eyes before, but the thought vanishes when I notice he has succeeded in capturing one of my hands within his own. I snatch it away before I know what I am doing, startled into blurting a bold question.

"Why do you stare at me that way?"

The young fey man is not bothered by it. He tilts his dark head to contemplate an answer. "You are beautiful, I think," he says slowly. "I was merely pondering the irony of lovely eyes with such sorrowful thoughts behind them."

I am not sure whether to be offended or embarrassed or glad that he has seen straight to my heart so easily. Settling for pride, I lift my chin a fraction and give a swift tug to my cloak.

"What do you know of my thoughts?" I mean for the words to sound haughty and am mortified when they come out sounding more like a plea.

"I know more of you than you think."

I draw my brows together. His words are perplexing, yet something deep within me wakes at the sound of them. I shake my head to clear it.

"I am late for home," I say by way of answer. "They will wonder where I am."

I take a step and my foot catches on something invisible upon the ground. I lurch forward, unable to catch myself. But the fey man's hand is already on my elbow, steadying me. In an instant, my head snaps up. His touch sends a shock through me. A muddle of memories collide in my mind.

I bend back to search the fey man's face for anything familiar. After some moments he laughs, as if my sharp gaze is amusing, and merely guides me into the trees without another word. I must trust that he knows the way, for I have nothing but the circle of blue lantern light to guide me through the dark, one faltering step at a time.

At the edge of the garden he stops and withdraws his arm from mine. My pride slinks away and falls between the cracks in the ground, and I find I am on the edge of begging for his hand again. Everything about him is familiar, even the warmth of our arms twined together.

One corner of his mouth quirks upward and I remember, too late, that he can read my thoughts. This time I refuse to be ashamed. I force myself to hold his gaze. For all I know, years could be passing while we stare at one another. His eyes jar me. They seem to hold more than the world in them. In the end, it is my gaze that drops first.

"I am home," I mumble, releasing him from any obligation he may feel to accompany me farther.

"Not your home, really," is his rather surprising reply. When he sees my small frown, he smiles. "I know you live here," he assures me. "But I think this place is not your true home."

I nod slowly. "It isn't. I was raised in the midlands, and came to the North but three years ago." But then, the fey folk followed me here, so he must know this already.

His brows lower a moment, as if my answer is not what he expects. But he says no more. He takes one of my hands in his, his touch as light as cobweb, and bows over it. As he bows, he looks up beneath his lashes at me and flashes that fey smile which makes my breath catch. Then he melts into the wood as if he is more a part of it than its own shadows.

The sound is so soft I barely hear it. In an instant I am sitting up in bed, straight as a poker. With a hiss, the covers fall from me and the cool night air brushes my skin. Something moves across the room in the shadows near the door. My heart trips as I remember the time the fey woman visited me once before on just such a night as this.

With a light step, a figure emerges into the wash of moonlight, and I see it is no fey creature, but Blessing. Her long nightgown whispers against the floorboards. Her golden curls are so beautiful that the moonlight reaches greedy fingers to grasp at them and turns them pale as hoarfrost. She wastes no time getting straight to the heart of her visit.

"Isidore, let us be friends again." The catch in her voice tells me she is choking on tears already.

I peer at her, too shocked to speak. Of all things, I did not expect this. She sees my hesitation and takes advantage of it. Quick as thought, she is at my bedside and my hand is within hers.

"Please. I am so alone, Iz, and I know you are, too."

For a moment, hope pushes at the walls of my heart. It is no more than the green knot on a winter branch, the promise of what will one day be a leaf.

Without warning, disgust sweeps down on that hope and chases it straight into the jaws of bitterness. I watch as its tender shoot is snapped to nothing.

I fling her hand from me like it is poisoned. I want to forget, but I cannot. I want to put everything behind us and be the sisters we truly are, but it is beyond me. It is too late. Has this not been proven enough? Hatred swells, strong as a riptide in my breast, and it is all I can do to get the next words out. The force of the past three years is in them.

"You took him from me."

"What?"

I swallow and try again. "You took Father from me."

Blessing cringes from the venom in my voice. Then she slowly lifts her chin and I know she is digging in her heels for this fight. "I didn't. It was you who turned from both of us. We beseeched you. I know you've not forgotten, so it's no use looking so shocked. We were as groveling as dogs, Father and Mother and I, begging for your love these past years. And you gave us nothing but coldness in return."

Her words are a knifepoint directed straight at my heart, and her aim proves pure and true. Fire flares beneath the surface of my skin. My cheeks are aflame. How does Blessing dare to argue about this? How can she compare her sorrow to mine?

I fling the covers aside and leap out of bed. Cold stings my bare feet as they hit the floor. Blessing skitters backward like a wary animal when she sees the fury in my eyes. As she does, her heel hits the bucket of ashes near the hearth. She flings her hands out and twists gracelessly sideways. With her arms at an awkward angle, she cannot catch herself, and goes sprawling. I hear the dull crack as her head hits the hearthstone. My stomach turns.

In the next moment, I am by her side. Already dark blood is pooling on the floor beneath her head. My hands flutter like ineffectual birds over the surface of her pale face. The overturned bucket is nearby and ashes hover like a cloud around me. Everything is covered in their fine, choking dust. Blessing's beautiful hair is caked with them. They have settled like murky snowflakes on her lashes.

"Blessing." I breathe her name like a charm that will make her eyes open, but it does not work.

"What's all this?" Hazel's voice comes from the doorway. Her silver brows are drawn together. Her gaze travels down to take in Blessing's form on the floor. Suddenly a terrible fear is written in the deep shadows of her face.

"Isidore, how did this happen?"

At first I do not understand her meaning. In the next moment I reel, for her words smack of accusation.

"You cannot think I did this?" I say. "She fell. She tripped. I didn't touch her." Our prattle is taking too long. "Hazel, she's injured—bleeding! Something must be done!"

Hazel nods. She believes me. She kneels upon the floor and lifts Blessing's head gently. The shawl slithers off her shoulders when she tugs at it. She wads it and presses it to the back of Blessing's head.

"Isidore, go for the physician," she says without looking at me. "Don't wake the servants, it will take too long. Go yourself. Hurry."

I do not bother to saddle my horse. It will take too much time. I do not even notice I am still in my nightgown until the sweat from my horse's back is slick on my bare legs. I ride with the black shadows of the forest on my left, and soon I am beating at the doctor's door. Dogs scrabble and howl on the other side and, in another moment, lantern light blooms beyond the curtains.

The doctor opens the door, his medical bag already in hand. He wastes no time to stop and speak, but bids me tell him what has happened while he readies his own horse. In a matter of minutes we are flying back along the path. But the physician's horse is fresh, and mine has made this journey once already, and at a furious pace. I soon fall behind. I do not care, so long as he arrives swiftly at Blessing's side.

The gardens sprawl ahead of me and I am just turning my horse to go around them when I hear it. I pull on the reigns and sit still, tilting my head. The sound comes from the wood and mingles with the shadows that stretch toward me. It is a strange song, with pain and beauty in it. Its notes pierce me to the heart like only one thing has ever had the power of doing.

Figures move between the trees, in and out of shadow and moonlight. When I strain to listen again for the fey song, I hear only a night hawk screaming a warning at its prey and, after that, only the wind running its fingers through the trees.

Though the song is gone, it still glints through the air and tingles across the surface of my skin. More than this, it has sunk to the deepest part of me. Perhaps it is knowing that Blessing may lie dying which brings the sudden burn of tears to my eyes. Perhaps it is merely that I realize now what I was prepared to throw away.

Love.

Again, I was ready to turn my back on it. Again. Despite the festered wounds left by bitterness, I was prepared to throw it aside. I am twice a fool.

Or was ready to be.

But the fey music has whispered something new, and now my heart drinks it in as if it has been dying of thirst for an age.

Love.

Just like that, Blessing is my sister once more. If she lives, I will never cast aside such a gift again. That I ever threw it away at all makes my heart ache with shame and grief.

I am not so dull that I do not see this for what it is. Another chance. Perhaps my last. I fix my gaze on the shadowy woods and make a fierce promise that I will not squander it.

Chapter Eight

*I*t is no use to deny Blessing's injury is a severe one, but the doctor assures us she will live. We must keep her in bed a fortnight, perhaps more. She is not to be moved under any circumstances. Head injuries are tricky things. He gives us thorough instructions as to her care and the food she must eat and not eat. I hang on every word, determined I will be the one to see her healthy again.

I stay by her side that first night, and when her eyes flutter open, minutes before sunrise, mine is the first face she sees.

"Iz?"

"I'm here."

Her fingers tremble at the edge of the bedclothes, and I reach to touch them.

"What happened?" She groans. "Why does my head feel so . . . strange?" Her lashes droop as if this handful of words is more than she has strength for.

"No, don't go to sleep," I say. "I've something to tell you."

My sister's eyes open again and she offers me a weak smile. "I already know what you will say, Izzy." The pressure of her hand is on mine, light as butterfly wings. I smile at her just as sleep draws his curtain between us.

But it is enough. I know that, against all odds, we have begun again.

I tell Blessing stories as she recovers. We talk a little, but when I see how this exhausts her I decide stories are safest. I tell her the tale of the proud, cruel lord who lost his way in the wood and emerged a century later to find his kin dead and gone. I tell her the tale of the fey prince who loved the human maid and took her to be princess of his kingdom. I tell her of the mortal king laid to rest in the fairy realm, ready to rise and fight for his people when the time grows ripe. And as I tell these tales and more, the cord which used to bind my sister and me together is taken up again from where it had lain, dusty and forgotten.

In the end I give up my most precious secret, the only one I ever kept from her. I tell Blessing of how I used to dance with the fey.

I think Blessing must be able to hear the longing in my voice. I can certainly feel it, heady as wine in my blood. When I speak of the glass slippers the fey women wear, she sits up in bed, eyes bright. I laugh at her and bid her lie down. She will have none of it. She insists on knowing what the slippers look like.

The whirl of fey feet dance back from my childhood, and the light streaming from the glint of glass that is delicate as cobweb. My mother's words sound in my mind. *With every step they take, they tread upon their own hearts.*

But that is what the slippers are, not what they look like.

So I say, "Moonlight."

Blessing sighs. "Moonlight . . ." she whispers to herself.

I smile. "Moonlight and prayers and glass and frost and wishes. That's what they look like."

"Oh, Isidore," she says. "It is a wonder you are still here and not searching for the entrance to the fey kingdom this very moment."

"I don't need to find their kingdom to get a pair of the shoes."
I pause for suspense and Blessing slaps my hand impatiently.

"Well, tell me, then!" she says.

"If one of the fey folk can be found on a night when the full moon shines down upon the snow, a wish may be claimed," I tell her as my heart begins to hammer my breastbone. "Why could the wish not be for a pair of glass slippers?" I direct the question to Blessing, though in truth I am asking myself. *And why not*, comes the swift answer.

Blessing is pale, and now I do insist that she rest. "The doctor will skin both of us if he knows you've excited yourself like this!" I scold, knowing full well it is my own fault for telling her this one last story. "Sleep a while and I will be back later with your supper."

When I step into the hall, Hazel is there. She gives a fine show of busyness with the tray in her hands, but I am not fooled. She has clearly been waiting for me. I question her with raised eyebrows and a half smile. She immediately abandons her pretense and pulls me to the bannister which overlooks the second floor corridor.

"There is to be a ball," she says without preamble.

I am sure Hazel expects more reaction from me than a shrug, but that is all I can muster. "And?"

My old nurse regards me narrowly. "And you will be going."

I am already shaking my head. "Oh, no. I have no wish to dance. And it is too soon—"

"Too soon to find a husband? You are seventeen, and so is your sister, for that matter. Plenty old enough for marriage."

She is being coy, for that is not what I meant and she knows it. I meant that it is too soon upon tragedy's heels to think of things like dancing at balls. Before I can say as much, I realize what she has suggested.

"A husband?" I give a scoffing snort. But when I see she is serious I take a step back. "*No*, Hazel."

"The young Lord Auren is seeking a wife," Hazel says, clutching at my arm and tugging me down the hall. "From all accounts he is a handsome and kind young man. You could do worse. Much worse." When Hazel sees the stubborn set to my jaw she continues, shrugging, "But if you want to wait a few years, go right ahead. There are plenty of rich men for the taking. Every one as old as I am, of course." She smirks. "But with fewer teeth."

I stop walking and Hazel halts next to me. "You should know better, Hazel," I tell her. "It will take more to cow me into marriage than threats of old, toothless men." But my mind is awhirl with the beginnings of an idea. "However," I continue before she can protest, "I will consider going."

Hazel's mouth sags open. She was clearly winding up for an argument, and I have taken the steam right out of her. At last she nods, studying me all the while as if she suspects me of trickery. Her suspicion is well founded, in fact, for there is more which I do not say aloud. I do not tell her that I will only consider attending this ball if Blessing is well enough to go, too. I do not tell her it is Blessing who should meet and love this young lord, and not I.

I do not say these things, for Hazel would only argue, and I have not the patience for it. My mind is set.

Blessing begins to recover quickly when she hears there is to be a ball. She has always had more heart for dresses and parties and the conversation of silly people than I. However, I am glad to see the paleness in her cheeks turn to a rosy bloom. She is still weak, but if we are careful she will be able to attend this ball.

The days grow colder as winter creeps across the North with the slow, unrelenting steps of a frosty giant. Yet the more the air chills, the merrier we are. I can scarcely believe the pathetic thing I was mere weeks ago. My sister has returned. I should want no more than this.

But somehow, to my shame, I do.

Despite my joy, there is yet an unnamed ache within me, so deep and subtle it is easy to ignore most of the time. I wonder if it is Father's death which causes it, for it is a blade in my heart I think I will never dislodge. Still, if I am honest, it feels like something even more than this. Surrounded by happiness and a bright future, now, unaccountably, I begin to lose my hold on hope.

It is not until the day before the ball that I think I understand the reason.

We are aflutter the whole day with final fittings and tryings-on of our gowns. I choose a shimmering taffeta that makes me think of the deep green pines in the wood. Blessing chooses a frothy silk, as blue as a morning sky. It is to be a masquerade, and countless hours have been spent deciding on the perfect masks.

I turn before my mirror, unable to reconcile the reflection with reality. In my mind I see the plump, round cheeks, the thick waist and the dimpled fingers of my girlhood. But the person looking at me is tall and slender and assured, nothing like the one I know still lives deep within me. Granted, I am not beautiful. My mouth is still too wide and is perhaps set in a more stubborn line than is considered attractive in young women of my age. At least, that is what Hazel often likes to remind me. Still, the overall effect leaves me gaping like a fool. Behind me, my old nurse clucks with approval.

"Oh, yes, my girl. What a beauty you've become. Who'd have thought it?"

I cringe at that word, *beauty*. Yet I smile, too. Hazel's old eyes see me through a filter fashioned of more love than truth, and I would not do without that for the world.

"Now the mask." Hazel lifts it gingerly from the gilded box on my bed.

The dull winter light coming weakly through my windows is enough to make this mask glow. I chose it from a multitude of others, yet the moment I saw it I looked no farther. It is pearly white, and one side is plain and without embellishment. From the other side sprout the wings of a swallowtail in the first leap of graceful flight. At first glance the wings appear white. In truth, they are a green so faint it is like the first timid steps of spring. Tiny emeralds are embedded along the edge of each wingtip. They wink and glimmer like things alive, and as I gaze at them the butterfly's wings appear to tremble with the eagerness to fly.

The mask is cool against my face. Hazel nods in solemn admiration. When she has stared long enough that I begin to get uncomfortable, I shoo her from the room.

"I can undress myself," I say, squeezing her hand in thanks.

The moment I am alone I turn from the mirror in relief. I can still feel the beauty of the gown and the mask itself flowing through me. *Perhaps*, I think, *they are enough to make me beautiful in truth*. My cheeks grow hot as I remember that the fey man called me beautiful. They grow hotter still when I recall how easily he saw the sadness within me.

I fling the mask onto my bed and cross the room to the window. I flip the latch and swing the shutters open wide. Air hits my face, cold as iron, and I know winter is well and truly here at last. I rest my elbows on the sill a moment, letting the chill air flood through me. That is when I feel it.

A cool kiss, soft as the brush of a butterfly wing, lands on my eyelid. I open my eyes just as another touches my nose, and another my lips.

I draw back from the window as if I have been struck.

No, not kisses. Snowflakes.

A turmoil of thoughts vie for my attention. One is louder than the others, and I reach out to snatch at it. As it dredges up from my memory, I see it is more of an image than a thought or a feeling.

Fairy wishes and full moonlight on the snow-covered ground. The image sinks in and my heart turns into a flock of panicked birds, flurrying and beating at my insides to be let free.

Tonight, I think. Tonight is the full moon. Tonight snow will cover the ground.

Tonight I will claim my wish.

Chapter Nine

It would be folly to tell anyone what I plan to do. Perhaps they would try to stop me or, worse, try to accompany me. I do not believe in my heart that Hazel or Blessing would do either of these things, but I am unwilling to take chances. Not with this.

At long last I think I understand what this emptiness in me has been. I have longed for these slippers for most of my life. When I am granted them tonight, perhaps they will fill the black space in my heart. I cannot wish for the thing I want more than anything else—my parents at my side. Even the fey could not do that. But perhaps the glass slippers will lead me straight to them, or work some other magic I cannot fathom. Who can tell?

Not for a moment do I believe they are ordinary slippers. No. I know that when I slip them on my feet, whatever comes next, I will never be the same. Never again will I make the mistakes I have made thus far in my life. I will be careful, for I will be treading upon my own heart.

I do not bother with a lantern. It would only betray me. Besides, the forest will be full to the brim with moonlight tonight. In no time I am beyond the gardens and at the edge of the wood. It is darker beyond the trees, but I can see my path well enough. Without hesitation, I step into the shadows.

Snow covers my head like a veil of white lace. It is thick on the ground and is falling in plump, twirling flakes around me. It revels and capers in and out of moonbeams, glorying in itself. For a moment, I want to dance with it.

But I have a task to do.

The clearing is as I remember. It has been some time since I have been to it, some time since I saw the folk standing in a solemn circle in the quiet of the night. In some part of me I recognize that this place is a sacred one to the fey. If I am to find them anywhere in the wood tonight, it will be here.

I settle behind a tree at the edge of the clearing and wait. It is not until I am startled awake that I realize I was sleeping at all. There is no noise, no echo of a noise, which could have wakened me with such force. But there is a humming in the air around me, a vibration through my bones. It has me on my feet in an instant.

The fey are here.

Their very bodies speak of silence. Their slightest movement is as soft as the snow gathering on their earthy cloaks. Though several of them stand scattered about the clearing, there is but a single pair of footprints in the snow. Every eye is leveled at one thing standing in their midst. That thing is a human.

It is Blessing.

My heart stumbles in confusion, then crashes headlong against my breastbone. Something squeezes at my lungs like a vice.

I watch Blessing from afar, speaking with the fey folk. Supplicating them, by all appearances. My belly lurches in rebellion as I watch the folk smile at her, their faces aglow. The woman nearest Blessing gives a subtle nod and slides a white hand within the folds of her cloak. From it she pulls a small satchel.

At the sight of the satchel, I freeze. My fingers dig into the bark of the tree I am leaning against. I think perhaps I am clawing too hard and should feel pain, but I cannot tell. My only thought is of that satchel, which Blessing takes from the fey woman's hands.

The folk are disappearing, their job apparently done. Blessing has had her wish from them and they have no reason to stay. By the time Blessing is left standing alone in the clearing, I am sinking to my knees. By the time she has opened the satchel to pull a single glass slipper from it, tears are freezing on my face.

But surely I am being foolish.

Blessing loves me as I love her, I know it. She would never get the slippers for herself. She would never take this wish from me, this one last thing I have shared with her from my heart. Perhaps, after all, she only wished for them so that she may give them to me.

Yet, even now, Blessing places the lone slipper upon the ground. She pulls her foot from the dainty boot she wears and slips it into the smooth glass. It fits as if it was meant for her. It fits as if she is beloved of the fey, and I am not.

I shudder with the knowledge that she has betrayed me. If nothing else convinces me, the smile on her face does so.

I watch her a moment longer as she pushes the slipper back into the bag and makes her way from the clearing toward home. Her smile may just as well be a knife thrown straight at my heart, for it gives me as much pain or more. I turn from the sight of her and from the anguish that twists through me like poison.

I wait for fury to burn its trail in me, but all I can feel is mourning.

My dreams that night are like churning, maddened waves during a storm. They are a disjointed tangle of grief. Hatred surfaces, that black thing I had thought vanquished, and this time it is different. Impure. It is diluted by love.

It should be a simple thing, hating Blessing after what she has done, yet I find it is not simple in the least. Love and hate are so tightly interlaced within me, it is impossible to separate them. I am no longer a blind child. I will no longer hate with such purity as I once did. It is different now, a muddled tug of war.

Part of me screams *trust*. And I long to obey it. But another part rises, as dark as a creature from the deepest part of the sea. And it whispers *revenge*. It is this voice, this dark voice, which seduces me. With a sense of doom and even satisfaction, I realize it is this voice I will obey.

When I wake I know I cannot have been sleeping long. My covers are tangled around me, mimicking the twist of the dreams I have just left behind. The night is frozen, as if time has come to a halt. The only thing moving is this dark thing in me. It whispers its poison in my ears, and I am too weak to fight it. I creep from my bed to answer its call.

My sister's door opens without a sound. I would not care if it screeched a warning and brought the whole household down upon us. Either way, I am bent on this plan.

My heart gives a painful lurch when I see Blessing lying there. She sleeps as soundly as if she has not just been wandering the forest like a gypsy, as if she has not just recovered from a grave injury. Her lovely face shows no trace of the guilt she should feel. I myself feel her betrayal so sharply I think it must be written in every move I make. How has she managed to escape it?

Seeing her thus makes me fear I will lose my resolve, so I quickly begin searching her room. It does not take long to find the slippers. She has not bothered to hide them. They are propped on the floor beneath her mirror. A wisp of translucent fabric barely covers them from view.

I squat beside them and reach out. My hand stops partway. After aching for these slippers so long, I am now reluctant to touch them. Fear sends stinging barbs across my skin. I shake my head angrily, denying it power over me, and thrust my hands out to seize the slippers.

My first thought is that they cannot possibly be made of glass. They are softer and smoother than glass, almost warm to my touch. When I told Blessing they were spun from moonlight, I was near the truth.

For a moment all else fades but their beauty. Even my anger and pain are gone as I contemplate what these slippers mean. What they are. They fairly pulse with life beneath my fingers. Rising, I dangle them before my face and gaze at them for several long moments. Do they hold my dreams, as I believed they might? My very heart? But perhaps these only hold Blessing's dreams, since they were given to her. I will never know.

Neither will she.

Before I can change my mind, I drag back my arm to throw the slippers across the room. I stifle a cry of astonishment as someone steps from the shadows near the window. My hand falls to my side, the slippers still clutched in them. It is the fey man. Gone is the playful youth that walked with me in the wood. His dark eyes are thunder and lightning. I remember how he heard my thoughts once before. There can be no doubt he has heard them now.

"Don't do this," he says without moving.

I whimper. It is pathetic, the sound a wounded animal might make. My glance shifts to Blessing. She is beautiful and serene in her slumber. The fey man need only look upon her face, as I am doing now, and I will become nothing to him. Indeed, all I have ever had are her leavings.

Grief has me by the throat. With a strangled cry, I throw the slippers as hard as I can. The noise they make when they shatter on the wall is as beautiful as music and as horrible as the breaking of a heart.

I feel the horror of what I have done even before I see the fey man's face. His anger is gone and a wretched pain floods his eyes, as if it is his heart I have just broken and not my own. Impulsively, I step forward, reaching for him. But moonlight and shadow swallow him up and he is gone. The place he stood is empty, but it is nothing compared to the emptiness that is within me.

"Izzy, what have you done?"

Blessing is sitting up in her bed, eyes wide. It takes her a moment to understand what has happened. She turns her head and catches sight of the glittering remains of the slippers, scattered across the floor, and puts a hand to her mouth. Before I know what is happening she has leapt from her bed and is across the room in front of me. Her hand flies out and she strikes me across the face. It does not hurt much, but I am brimful of fury all the same.

"How dare you?" I hiss. "How could you do such a thing to me?"

She gives a guttural laugh. "Funny. That's what I was going to ask you."

My anger is nearly choking me now. "Oh, yes," I say. "How could I destroy something of yours? How could I take something from *you*, do you mean?" I nearly spit in her face. Has she no shame, to stand here and blame me for the very thing she has done time and again?

"You knew I wanted them," I continue, horrified to hear the tremble in my voice. "You knew they were meant to be mine. How could you . . ." I sound like a child crying for a toy. For all I know, that is exactly what I am. This wound I thought healed was only festering beneath the surface all these years. Now it is split open and spilling poison everywhere.

Blessing has always possessed what I want. Beauty, grace, the love of my father. And now she has stolen the last thing, the sole thing I wished for.

Or thought I wished for.

The glass slippers are broken and gone, and I will never wear them. But the moment they shattered on the floor, they dissipated from my mind and from my heart. In this moment all I can think of is the fey man's face as he disappeared into shadow, and that I may never see him again.

I see now the fatal flaw in revenge. It turns sour the moment it is exacted. I am sick with it, right down to my bones. I may have hated Blessing when she took Father from me, but since then something has changed. I can never hate her again. Not even after this. Perhaps the fey man knew that. Perhaps that is what makes this sin of mine worse than any other I have yet committed. For I have not turned my back on love, as I did once before, but betrayed it while yet holding it close.

"You little fool," Blessing says, and there is something close to helpless laughter in her voice. "Oh, Iz, you don't know what you've done, do you? You can't think I got the slippers for myself."

"I saw you try one on." My accusation is quick as lightning.

Blessing is unfazed by it. "Of course I did. They were utterly beautiful, just as you told me they would be. Who could resist it? But trying them on and keeping them are two wholly different things."

As Blessing squats on the floor, her gown billows around her like a cloud. With careful fingers she picks up one piece of the broken glass. And it is glass, I can see that now. Nothing more. Those slippers could never have held a heart, least of all mine. Why then, I wonder, does it feel as if the pieces of my fractured heart are lying on the floor with them?

"They were yours," she whispers. "I got them for you." She rises and her next words flare with anger. "You've always seen the worst in things. Well, are you happy now? You've broken the slippers like a spoiled child, and they were yours all along. You were too selfish to see what would have been obvious to any simpleton—that I would never have taken them for myself. But you preferred to destroy them rather than to see anyone else so much as touch them."

Her words are so bright and harsh that I have to blink. The truth of them shatters inside of me, sending shards of light and pain straight into my heart. For she is right. I have broken everything which has ever been given to me, simply because it was not perfectly to my taste. It is a horrible truth to swallow. I fear it will poison me if I try.

"Isidore." When I hear the tenderness in Blessing's voice I realize I am crying. But when she approaches I back away.

"No." This one last wound is too fresh, even if it is of my own doing. If I speak of it now I will surely bleed to death.

"But—"

"No." I shake my head, putting all the resolve I can muster into my voice. Blessing's mouth shuts like flower petals closing, and she gives me a look I cannot fathom.

In my own bed I curl into a ball. I cannot even gather the strength to crawl beneath the covers. I think of the handful of words the fey folk have spoken to me here in the North. They sounded like comfort when they were first spoken. Now I fight the urge to see them as accusations.

Though if I am honest, I must admit them for simply the truth.

I remember the fey woman's whisper to me the night she wove Dewdrops into my hair.

Do not lose your heart.

The memory of broken glass thrusts its sharp corners deeper into my heart and I curl tighter, cowering. *Do not lose your heart,* she said. What she did not tell me was that the surest way to lose it was to hold it tight.

Softer still come the fey man's words.

This is not your home.

No, I want to answer him, *it is not and never has been.* I am wandering here, and lost. This world fits me like an ill-made garment, and I cannot help but dream of a time I might cast it aside to don one made to measure for me.

When I remember the anguish in the fey man's face, I know the slippers are not the only things that I have broken this night. The slippers would only have been a balm to cool the fire of this sickness I carry. They could never have healed it.

Only one thing can do that.

So it is now, in my coldest and loneliest of moments, that I fathom the emptiness that has been in me for so long. More so, I know at last the one way to fill it.

In the same moment that I learn what I truly desire, I understand that it is too late. For I have already destroyed it.

Chapter Ten

I cannot imagine a heavier silence than the one hovering between my sister and me as we rumble down the road to the ball. Within the walls of the coach, the atmosphere is so thick it is difficult to draw breath. We sit pressed against opposite corners of the coach like two hostile cats, prepared at any moment to bring out claws. Blessing's eyes flash blue fury at me from behind her pearl-encrusted mask, and I do the best I can to stave off the roil of emotions washing over me. Guilt and shame are high among them.

Lord Auren's abode is more palace than house. We can see it shining, brimful of candlelight, from a mile away, as if the sun is preparing to rise in the west. Its tall stone towers and sweeping verandas are too grand for my taste. I would take a cottage in the heart of the wood before I would think of living in such a place as this. But from the corner of my eye I see Blessing grow still, and from the way her slender shoulders rise and fall I know she is breathless with awe.

The wide front doors are thrown open and light spills from them and from the windows. It stretches its golden fingers down the stone steps and onto the frost-covered lawn. We enter the doors together and I melt into the crowd as soon as I can, with only a slight stab of guilt at leaving Blessing alone. Even with her mask in place, she is far and away the loveliest woman here tonight, and soon she is surrounded by men petitioning her to dance.

Giving an inward scoff, I turn my attention to my surroundings. The ballroom is stunning on the merit of its size alone. Thick columns of marble rise so high that the light from the multitude of candles cannot find the top of them. Evergreen boughs and holly branches, bright with berries, are hung everywhere, giving the hall a festive, intimate quality I would not have thought possible in a room so vast.

And everywhere, everywhere, are masked people. Couples hop and twirl past me in a galliard while the scent of perfume accosts my nose. Their masks are a wonder to see. I marvel at the intricacy of some and cringe at the ferocity of others. There is an owl with feathers poking out from every side and the slash of a sharp beak down the center. There is a man with a face of green leaves fanning out from his eyes. There are gilded masks and jeweled masks and masks of lace and ribbons and animal hide.

As I stand among the crush of guests, wishing already for this night to be over, a strange feeling comes over me. Like the whisper of a breeze, it touches the base of my neck and the tips of my ears. A shiver creeps under my skin as I turn slowly around.

It takes me a moment to pick him out. When I do, there is no doubt his gaze is fixed on me. A man is standing across the room. It is a wonder I can see him, for the crowd swarms thick between us. Beneath his mask I can see the angle of a pale, strong jaw. The mask itself is made of burnished metal, thin as parchment, and it angles gracefully around the sides of his face. The eye holes are filled with darkness, and only a glint of dancing light convinces me there are eyes behind them at all. Extending upward from the mask is a pronged diadem. It is a crown fit for a king, and I wonder at the boldness of any man who would wear such a thing in the house of a great lord. Unless . . .

I tap the person next to me and the face of a wolf, fangs bared, looms above me. "Excuse me," I say. "Where is Lord Auren?"

"Young Auren? Hm, let's see." Though the mask is fierce, its wearer is nothing but a portly old man, his round belly poking out like a drum before him. He gives me a kind smile before he scans the crowd. "I saw him not long ago, but there's little doubt he is skulking in the shadows somewhere. Auren hates balls, poor lad."

"Do you know what mask he is wearing tonight?" I cast another glance to where the man with the crown had been standing. He is gone. I give a small huff of frustration. "Was he masked as a king?" I venture.

"Who, Auren?" The man gives a bellowing laugh. "Not he! A king! Oh, what a thought. It's a wonder he's even wearing a mask. He doesn't like drawing attention to himself, you see. I saw him not a few minutes since. Hmm, what was he wearing?" He turns to the lady at his side, whose face is masked in black starched lace. "Belle, my dear, what mask was the young lord wearing? A crimson dragon, was it not?"

"A crimson dragon?" The lady frowns and gives him a sharp rap on the shoulder with her fan. "Nothing like. It was gilded blue, encrusted with diamonds."

They begin to bicker and I quickly thank them and duck away through the crowd. It seems I must find Auren myself. I am eager to reassure myself that the young lord and the man in the crowned mask are not the same person, though I cannot say why.

In the end, it is Blessing who leads me to him. If I had given half a moment's thought to it, I could have guessed as much, for fully half the men in the room are buzzing about her like hummingbirds around a flower. Why should Auren not be there, too?

But if she is a flower, she is surely a wilting flower. Her mask cannot hide the look of a trapped animal I see in her eyes. I wonder how the men speaking with her do not see it. I fight the urge to push through them and whisk her away to a place where we can both gossip and laugh over the people in this fanciful, foolish place.

There is a rustling sound to my left, and I twist around in time to see a man making his way through the crowd of others. His steps are slow, like a man who has stumbled into a dream. His mask is a simple white and covers one side of his face. The other side shows skin that is soft and youthful. His eyes and hair are brown as a doe's. He is hardly more than a boy, yet when the others fall silent and make way for him, I realize I have found the young lord at last.

Auren offers Blessing a polite bow and extends his arm for her to take. Without a word, he leads her from her group of admirers and across the room. I follow in their wake at a distance, using the bright banner of Blessing's golden hair to guide me through the throng.

They disappear behind the thick curtains of a window alcove and I want to stomp with annoyance, for I had hoped to spy a while longer. Instead, I tuck myself as close to the wall as I can get and put my ear against the curtain. It is shameless, I suppose, but I am beyond caring.

"Thank you." Blessing's voice is a wisp of sound. She is breathless with some emotion. It sounds half fear and half elation.

"It's no trouble." There is a smile in Auren's voice. "I will admit, I was perhaps being more selfish than gallant by rescuing you. I've watched you the night through and knew I couldn't let you leave until I met you."

I can almost feel the heat of Blessing's blushing cheeks from my side of the curtain, so certain am I of her reaction. This is the moment another girl might simper or play coy. Yet, despite her discomfort, I hear Blessing say, "I have no need for such praise. This much and more has been spoken to me too many times to count tonight. I am weary of it." There is a note of impatience in her voice. I cannot help but admire her for it.

"I'm glad to hear it," Auren says cheerfully. "I was hoping you were not that kind of girl. I had to be sure, of course."

I press closer into the curtain, my interest piqued.

Blessing gives one of her tinkling laughs. "Well that makes things much easier, though I wouldn't have you think I'm ungrateful that you stepped in when you did. I'm not used to so many people as this. My sister and I live alone, you see, and our lives are very quiet and simple."

"Alone? You've no parents, then?"

"My mother and stepfather died four months ago." The sorrow that is sharp in Blessing's voice echoes in my own chest. Auren is quick to respond to it.

"I am sorry," he says. "What a horror for you. We don't have to speak of it if it will cause you pain. My own father died a year ago. It is hard to move on," his voice lowers a fraction, "but not impossible."

So in a matter of moments they move from formal to intimate, and I hear their talk continue as if they are childhood friends who have just been reunited. I step away from the curtain and shake my head. After everything, here is Blessing once again, ready to pluck happiness as if it is a bright flower which has sprung up just for her. I am frozen with warring emotions, torn between wanting to rejoice with my sister at this unexpected gift and wanting to trample its delicate petals beneath my feet.

This had been my plan, of course. Dear Hazel had thought I would be a match for Auren, but I had known better. Who better fit to be the wife of a lord than Blessing? I had wished this for her. I had planned it.

Swift on the tail of this thought comes another darker one. An image of Blessing slipping her foot into the fey slipper. Then another, from a deeper place, of her hand lying contently in my father's.

Am I to let this happen? How easy it would be to snatch this happiness out from under Blessing, just as it has been snatched from me so many times. My heart beats a wild, unsteady rhythm as I press to the curtain once more. Blood rushes in my ears.

"I will certainly take my mask off," Blessing is saying. "But I will not do it alone. You must take yours off at the same time."

"Very well." Auren's voice shakes with amusement. Perhaps it is the first time he has felt joy since his own father died. My resolve wobbles sideways.

"Are you ready?" Blessing's voice is teasing. "One." She draws out the number as she says it, and I hear Auren snort with laughter. They are, after all, but two children together. "Two."

My fingers are slick with sweat as they grip a fold of the curtain. I am ready to rip it aside and stop this nonsense, but somehow I am waiting a second longer, and then another.

"Three!"

Their laughter dies to silence as, behind the curtain, they gaze on one another's unmasked faces. I have missed my moment and now I am nothing but an intruder. I am keenly aware I have stepped into a sacred circle, a place I have no right to be. My face is hot and my eyes are burning with inexplicable tears.

Truth hits me with the force of a storm.

I am not that person. I do not have to be that person ever again. I do not need to break the happiness of others merely because it is not my own. Perhaps I once was that girl, but something has changed in me. A seed born of fey music and broken glass pushes at my heart, tiny but stubborn, and I know for a certainty that I am new.

I step back from the curtain and bump into something solid. Someone.

"You see," a voice says, close to my ear. "I knew this place was not your home."

The words catch like a barb in my heart, so close are they to what I feel already. I gaze up into the face of the one who spoke them. The man wearing the crowned mask looks back at me. Behind the thin layer of iron his dark eyes are two shining stars. My breath comes in quick, shallow spurts. I thought I would never see him again.

He does not give me time to respond. His fingers are already woven through mine as he says simply, "Will you dance?"

My blood races like quicksilver through my veins as he leads me to the center of the floor. But he does not stop there. We go straight through the crowd of people with their frills and baubles and masks, onto the veranda beyond. Yet even here we do not stop. The chill wind catches at the edges of his long cloak and at the rim of my gown as we descend the stone stairs and step onto the lawn.

On this side of the house no lanterns are lit. There is only the moon to guide our steps. The frosty grass sparkles like a thousand glittering diamonds spread before our feet. It is this, then, that is to be our ballroom. Already he is lifting my hand and bowing low. My nerves run smooth at that, and I let go a breath which is part laughter and part bliss. I offer a curtsy in return, and we begin.

The steps to this dance are like none they will be dancing inside. These steps are a part of me. This dance is the dance of my childhood. The music, unfurling gently toward us from some-where beyond the shadows, sends shivers of recognition down my spine. We leap and whirl, our feet as light as wishes, as we dance a fey jig. A night such as this should send cold straight to my bones, but I cannot feel it while I touch his hand.

As I dance, something strange happens. Each step I dance is a step backward for my heart, and by the time we are finished, breathless and smiling, it is once more the heart of a child. I have danced back to my childhood. I have found the path and returned to the place I began. The glass slippers are gone from my mind, as if they had never been. I do not need them. I think perhaps I never did. It must be a miracle, a miracle that should set the ground trembling and change the very colors of the sky. Yet it happens quietly, as sweetly as a flower opening. I am left quivering and weak from the sheer joy of it.

I hardly dare to bring sorrow to this perfect moment, but I know it must be done.

"The slippers . . ." I do not finish, but he understands.

"They were nothing," he says.

"Nothing?" I cannot fathom it, for I saw the heartbreak on his face when they shattered. "But I destroyed them."

"The slippers were nothing," he repeats. "I only wished to stop you from destroying something more precious to me still."

My voice falters a little as I ask, "And what was that?"

"Yourself." He shakes his head as if he cannot believe I need to be told.

When he reaches to draw me close, I do not resist. It would be as foolish as refusing air into my lungs. We stay twined together for the space of twelve heartbeats before he speaks.

"Do you remember, I wonder?" His breath is warm on my hair.

"Remember?"

"Me. Do you remember me?"

I draw back and lift my gaze to meet his. He reaches to lift his mask. I have seen the fey man only a handful of times and already his face is as familiar to me as my own. But only in this moment do I understand why. I have known him all my life. The veil lifts from my memories and the truth dazzles my eyes.

"You," I breathe. "You were there. When I danced in the glade with the others. When I was a child."

He dips his head in a bow of assent. I can see from the small quirk at the corner of his mouth that he is pleased I know him.

"And it was you who helped me the time I fell. It was your hand that lifted me and held me close." I look at him with new eyes, my heart beating fast. "You didn't dance, though." I frown as the memory uncurls in my mind. "You watched the rest of us from your place at the edge of the clearing, yet you never joined us. Not once." I pause. "Why?"

"Can you not guess?" He tilts his head in a way which is becoming familiar to me. "You were but a child, then, as you say. Yet I loved you. The moment you were born, I felt your presence. Even across the divide of our two worlds, it jarred me to the core. You were for me, more to me than even the blood in my veins. And I have loved you since that day. I have only been waiting these years for you to be ready to love me in return." The look he gives me is rippling and deep, as palpable as a caress, and my ears are burning from its passion. "I would not dance with anyone," he says, "until I could dance this dance, tonight, with you."

I remember myself as a child, pudgy and awkward and unsure of myself. For a moment I wonder how anyone could love such a child as that, let alone the woman she promised to become. My wonder lasts only an instant, then it is gone. For I cannot deny any of this. The truth of it is radiant in his face, as powerful as a wave that threatens to drown me.

My shoulders shiver and a lifetime of sorrow drops from them like an unwanted skin. With a boldness that leaves me breathless, I stretch on tiptoe and press my mouth to the fey man's in a quick, hard kiss of joy. His lips turn upward beneath mine as he smiles, and his arms come around me. But I slip out of his embrace with a laugh and knit my fingers through his once again. There will be time enough for embraces later, and I fully intend to make use of it.

For now, I want to dance. My feet are restless to join the music I hear all around me.

Chapter Eleven

It is the early hours of morning when I step into the coach. The world is awash with a foggy gray light and the moon is paling in a winter-white sky. I pull the lacy curtain from the coach window and see people everywhere, flooding the veranda and the wide stone steps, preparing to leave the ball.

Among the departing crowd I spot Blessing. Her arm is wound through Lord Auren's. Their masks are nowhere to be seen, doubtless lying forgotten in the shadows of a window alcove. The glow on their faces is enough to make me blink, as if the sun has just peeked from behind a cloud. They descend together and he helps her into the coach, though it is clear neither of them wishes to release the other's hand.

As Blessing steps into the carriage, she gives a little twist and puts a hand to her mouth. Her shoe hits the graveled drive with a soft plink. In an instant, Auren bends to retrieve it.

"I'm so clumsy," Blessing says by way of apology. But her smile is playful.

"Here, sit down," Auren commands. "I will help you put it on. You *are* clumsy, aren't you?" he teases as his eyes sparkle at her.

Blessing shakes her head. "Keep it. Then you will be forced to visit when you return it to me." She tilts her head to the side. "I think I will need it soon. Tomorrow, in fact."

I lift my hand to hide my smile. I can scarcely believe this brazen sister of mine.

Auren makes a mock scoffing sound. "Forced? What's this? Do I seem false-hearted, that you must *force* me to visit you?"

Neither of them spares me a glance, they are so lost in this foolish lovers' banter. But I am not the same person I was mere hours ago, and I do not begrudge them a moment of it. When Blessing leans into the coach and the door is shut at last, she turns to me at once. The fire in her gaze nearly knocks me backward.

"Izzy, forgive me."

I am startled into silence. She has spoken the very words on my own lips.

"Once, I blamed you for being an unworthy daughter," she says. Her face gives a small spasm of shame. "I never gave a thought to how unworthy of a sister I was to you."

This is too much for me. "Blessing—" I begin, but she lifts a hand to silence me.

"You were right," she says. Tears make her eyes glitter like jewels. "I wanted your father for my own, you know. I threw over our friendship for it. I was ashamed of how badly I wanted him to be my father, and . . . and not yours." She sniffles. "Yet somehow, the whole time, I loved you just the same. I swear I did."

I am nodding already, for I understand. In fact, I think there is no one on earth who understands better than I. I take a breath and prepare to plunge into the darkness of my own regrets and confessions. Blessing anticipates me.

"Please don't, Izzy." Her touch is delicate on my hand. "I know. I know you're sorry, too. And I understand why you did the things you did. I do, truly. Please don't apologize to me. Let us be sisters once more, that's all I ask."

My smile is sad, for Blessing has done it again. It is the last thing she steals from me, this apology, and it is perhaps the most painful. Yet I nearly get to my knees and thank her, because the last tattered fragment of truth has fallen into place.

Everything I ever believed stolen from me was only something being given, something being shared which I did not wish to share myself. I did not wish to share Blessing with Father, I did not wish to share Father with Blessing, and I did not wish to share the fey slippers with anyone at all.

I was the breaker of my own heart, time and again. I did not need the fey slippers to tread upon it, for I have been treading on my heart these many years already, shattering it bit by bit in the clutch of my own grasping fingers.

Though relief washes through me, a thin vein of something else is there, too. It is the one last truth I uncover. The truth I think everything else has been buried within for the whole of my life.

I can never be whole. I do not belong here.

I am not home.

It is an emptiness that resounds in me, demanding to be answered.

Yet something else trickles in between the cracks of this despairing thought. The hope of finding something to fill that emptiness. The hope that, perhaps, I have found it already. And suddenly hope is a thing alive, soaring in me. Its wings beat against my ribs, wild with the promise of joy.

I take Blessing's hands in mine. For all that I thought we were sisters before, this is the moment we are sisters in truth. Pain and sorrow and heartbreak draw us close. Our wounds bleed together and make us true kin.

My happiness at reclaiming this gift at last is tinged with a dark slash of grief, for I now know I must leave it behind.

The household already begins to stir. The maids are in the hall, hiding their yawns as they poke at the hearth fires to get them roaring again. Blessing and I go straight to our rooms. At our doors, we stop to give each other a last look down the length of the corridor. We smile and say goodnight at the same instant, which makes us both laugh. Hazel is behind us, shooing us into our rooms.

"Stop your girlish nonsense, the two of you," she says. "Get to bed and sleep as long as you like. After a night like this one, you'll certainly need it. Ring for lunch when you wake and I'll send it up." She squints at me. "I'll be up with it, mind, for I intend to hear about everything that happened at that ball."

I roll my eyes at Blessing and she giggles. Impulsively, I rush down the hall and throw my arms around her. It is both an act of headlong childish love and of sorrowful farewell. I think she must feel it, for when we part she searches my face as if looking for something she cannot quite understand.

When the door to my room is closed, I shed my gown quickly and lay it on my bed. I slip into my simplest dress and throw a heavy cloak over my shoulders. I glance a last time about the room, which is flushed with rising sunlight, then step lightly out my door and into the corridor once again.

I jump backward, heart pounding, when I come nose to nose with Hazel. For a moment I think she will scold me as she takes in my appearance. Then I see her face. It is wretched with sadness and old beyond her years. She does not say a word. It is clear she understands what I mean to do.

"Oh, Hazel," I say, biting back the sob that rises in my throat. As I take her hand, regret pierces me. "If I could tell you what I feel, what this is . . ." I begin. But something changes in her face again.

"I tried." Her voice quivers. "I tried to make you fit in. I tried to make you happy here." She puts a wrinkled hand to her breast. "I think I always knew you did not belong. From the moment I came to your father's house and saw your wild eyes and the fiery heart that hid behind them . . . I just knew." Hazel smiles at me. Her old face becomes lovely with the brilliance of that smile. "It doesn't matter where you go. My love won't be stopped from following you there." She lifts her chin, daring me to gainsay her. I stand still, not sure I can tear my eyes from her beloved face. But she swallows, gives me a little shove, and says, "Go."

As I pass Blessing's door, I trail my fingers across the chiseled wood of it. I can almost feel the warmth of her dreams on the other side, pulsing and alive. They will all be for Auren now, and I wish her joy with every part of my heart.

Once I am in the garden I do not bother bridling my feet any longer. The hood of my cloak falls back as I dash down the frosted garden paths and plunge into the forest. Night is sloughing from the world and the rising sun flings a glittering luster through the trees. In no time I am deep within the wood. My feet find the familiar path on their own and soon I am standing at the clearing. It is empty but for a doe grazing on the acorns that peep from the snow, and she skitters away the moment she hears the crunch of my feet.

Just as I am wondering if I have been rash to come here, just as I suspect I have been foolish to think this possible, I see him. He appears in the glade as if he has stepped straight from one of the beams of sunlight spilling between the trees. It is the first time I have seen him in daylight, and suddenly I am shy. He has to beckon to me before I am willing to enter the glade myself.

Each step I take toward him is one more step closer to home. The truth of it sings in my blood and tingles across the surface of my skin. The wild thing that was in me, flapping its wings to escape, has quieted.

"Welcome to my wood," he says, holding a hand out to me.

I cannot say a word in answer. I can do nothing at all, in fact, but stare at him. In the light of the day, I see that his face is a world. And it is not just any world, but my world. Father and Mother are there, Hazel and Blessing and forests and streams and moonlight and wishes and even slippers made of glass.

Yet each of these things is only a drop which splashes into the ocean of the rest of him, for he is more, so much more than that. The filter of dusky sunlight pirouettes for a single moment, and as I peer through its glare I think I see a glittering crown upon the fey man's head. But then I blink and the crown is gone, and his face is once more the one I know. His dark eyes and hair are shining, and that quirk is tugging at the corner of his mouth. He is a boy again, as I am a girl.

"You understand?" he says. It is the vastest question I have ever been asked, but I am ready with a sure answer.

"Yes."

He tips his chin up and laughs, a sound like water over smooth stones. I see he is relieved, as if he thought that, even now, I might change my mind. But I never will. I never can. This world has not been a home to me, as he has told me before. As I have always known.

The trees arch at the edge of the glade, leaning together like lovers whispering secrets. I think I can hear their voices murmur as we walk hand in hand beneath their frosty branches. All around me the forest is changing, and I lift my head to gaze at it. It is the same, yet different. It is a brighter, more beautiful version of itself. Its colors are so deep and so sharp I must blink back tears from the piercing light of them. Its scents of earth and pine and frost are as near to me as my own skin. I wonder if they have become a part of my skin, or perhaps I am becoming a part of them. There is no way to tell.

And everywhere is music. Fey flutes and tambourines and fiddles drift on the chill breeze. The folk emerge from the shadows, gathering for a dance here on their side of the sunlight, here in their own realm.

"Will you dance?" The fey man says to me, as he has once before.

I hesitate only a moment. My chin brushes my shoulder as I turn for one last glance at the world I leave behind. It is growing dull and colorless already, as small as the infant's gown I grew out of long years ago.

"What do *you* think?" I say playfully, and my heart leaps at the white flash of his smile.

His fingers are cool as they slide between mine. He leads me to where the other fey have already begun their whirling and singing and merriment.

Yet before we begin, there is one last thing I must say. In truth, it is the only thing I should ever have said all my life. My mouth should have said it, my hands should have shown it, my feet should have danced it, and my heart should have sung it. At long last, here is my chance.

I stretch on tiptoes and place my lips against his ear. I whisper the words, and when I lean back I see that his eyes have already answered in kind. It is enough. For the first time in my life, it is enough. That is when I know I am home.

The light behind me shifts as the archway of trees comes together and the door to the old world is closed. But I do not give it another thought. Already my feet are flying as they dance down this bright new path.

The Word Changers
A Novel by Ashlee Willis
An Excerpt

Chapter One

A Bewildering Beginning

The moment she began to fall, Posy forgot everything except her descent. She even forgot how she had come to be falling in the first place. Everything behind her grew faint and far, and everything in front of her seemed a black void. Gravity worked backward, and her racing speed slowed. Now she floated, like a dry leaf, or a page torn from a book. Gradually she felt nothing at all.

And the entire time she was falling, she could hear voices, hollow and wide-flung, pulling her back from the precipice. Posy lifted a heavy hand to swat awkwardly at her face.

"You've come at last, my dear," said the voice nearest her. "And about time, too." Posy attempted to open her eyes, only to find it difficult. Was that the brush of a feather on her brow? She groaned in frustration at the weighted feeling she couldn't shake.

A woman's voice came faintly from a distance. "Will it work?"

"Well, their looks are quite different, I must say." Now a man's deep tones.

"It was what Your Majesty wanted, if I may remind you," the answer came smoothly. "And after all, it is much too late now to send her back."

"Let us hope it is only for a short time," the woman spoke again, with a slight accent of distaste. "But see. The princess begins to wake."

Why are they speaking so strangely? Posy's thoughts crawled sluggishly into her head. *And it is almost as if they are speaking about me . . . Did someone just say . . . 'Princess'?*

Only last night—was it last night?—Posy lay in her own bed, listening to the sounds of unhappiness down the hall. Crying hadn't stopped her parents from arguing. Praying hadn't ended their hate for each other. Fists clenched into the pillow she pulled over her head had done no good either. Of course it hadn't.

All the same, something deep within her had clamored and quaked for a change. Something inside had whispered that things could not remain as they were. Perhaps this was the answer. But she thought it more likely it was all a horrid mistake.

Solid arms went around her, pulling her to a sitting position. "There we go, my dear," said a man's voice next to her ear. "What a scare we had, didn't we, Valanor? We thought we were going to lose our princess."

There was no doubt about it now. Someone was calling her princess. Posy's eyes snapped open at last. What she saw almost convinced her she was dreaming, if everything hadn't been so real and so unbearably bright. She had not seen a place like this before. What had she been doing before all this happened? Why could she not remember?

Standing around her bed were several individuals. The first one she noticed was a large man, tall and broad, with ruddy cheeks and a full black beard streaked with shots of gray. His must have been the arms that had moved her, as easily as a doll, up on the bed. He was smiling broadly at her through small, intent eyes as he rubbed his hands together with the anticipation of someone a fraction his age. Next to him stood a tall slender woman, breathtakingly—*coldly*—beautiful. Her white-blond hair fell over her pale shoulders and shimmered like fairy dust down the back of her exquisite gown. Posy blinked at the sight of the gold crown on each of their heads. A group of people—servants from the look of it—surrounded the two of them, all peering curiously at her. *Just as the students in biology class all stare at those poor frogs in their glass tanks,* Posy thought with a grimace.

"Did . . .?" she began hesitantly. "Did someone call me— Princess?"

"Indeed! And how are you, my dear?" the man said, who seemed to be the king.

"I—I—am all right, I guess. Although—"

"Ah, good!" he boomed before Posy could say more. His grin widened, his white teeth gleamed. "Nothing to put you down for long, eh, Daughter?"

"Daughter?" Posy murmured in confusion, looking from the king to the queen and back again. She bit back a panicked laugh.

A vision of her own mother and father—nothing like these two—swept through her head and was gone. What *had* happened? she demanded of herself harshly. But she could remember nothing clearly. Nothing but . . . but . . . Posy sighed in frustration. The memory was just beyond her grasp.

"Yes, my daughter," the queen repeated, her rich voice filling the corners of the room. "You had a fever, and we have been worried about you these many days. We even feared for your life. But you have proved the doctors wrong and are on the mend at last."

"No," Posy shook her head, "I'm not your—"

"You may not remember, Princess," a smooth voice, neither the king's nor the queen's, cut in. "They say a fever can chase many memories away, even keep some away forever. You were on a hunt with your father and mother, the king and queen, and the lords and ladies of the court. It began to rain. You, being the excellent horsewoman you are, decided the rain would not stop the hunt. You pushed on. But alas, that very night when the hunting party returned, you took ill with a delirious fever and have been abed ever since. You have regained consciousness only today."

Posy heard these words with astonishment as she looked around the room for the person who had spoken them. At last, her eyes alighted on the stone windowsill. On it sat a great gray owl, at least twice the size an owl ought to be, sitting with feathered chest thrust forward, a self-satisfied expression on his face. Surely, she thought, to herself . . . surely the *owl* didn't just . . . But even as she doubted it, the creature spoke again.

"But now, here you are," he said soothingly, as if he were calming a distressed child, "and we all rejoice that you are restored to us."

Posy stared, open-mouthed, but the creature merely gazed back at her placidly from where he perched.

"Yes, yes," bellowed the king rather impatiently. "So we will leave you to rest, my dear. Come, Valanor." He took the queen's hand. "The Kingdom awaits us, you know." And they swept from the room.

The Kingdom awaits us? Posy snorted under her breath. Had the man really just spoken those words? They seemed theatrical—like those you'd hear in a fairytale, or read in a . . . Posy froze.

"In a book," she said aloud, though the room was now empty.

Memory flooded her then. Once again, she could hear her parents down the hall, just as she had countless times before. Their voices rose and fell in anger, traveling through the ouse and into her room like an endless, waking nightmare. She remembered the heavy tread of her own feet as she launched from her bed, heard the jarring of her parents' bedroom door as she ripped it open. And she had screamed at them—screamed to stop them shouting at one another, screamed to quiet the fear and anger that reared up inside her. But she had seen their faces turn toward her, and their expressions had gone from shock to anger and then a disappointed sadness that was worst of all.

"How dare they?" Posy turned sideways and whispered into her pillow. "How dare they get angry. They were the ones hurting *me*. And hurting Lily, too."

Posy felt a thrill of sorrow, thinking of her little sister. Lily was only eleven. To Posy's 15-year-old mind that was much too young to be subjected to the bitter misery of what their parents' marriage was doing to their family. She had hoped Lily had heard nothing of the wild interchange of that night, when her parents shouted cruel words at one another, and she shouted cruel words to them in turn.

Tears pricked behind her eyes. Yes, she remembered now. Anger and tears had etched such deep grooves into her young heard that she hated the very thought of them. Anger and tears were what drove her out of the house and straight down the street to the library. Peace, and silence, and books. Posy clung to these things.

And that was where she had discovered the book. She had found it innocently enough, she supposed. The library was an old one, to be sure, but she had thought she knew all its dusty corners and sagging shelves by now. But somehow, yesterday, she had found herself in an unfamiliar place. And down the dimly-lit aisle she had chosen a strange, musty book, with a scrolling, antique font. Posy had chosen it for the lettering. It had reminded her of the covers of the fairytales she had read as a child—the ones that made her feel like a character in a kingdom far away from any troubles she knew in her own world. And she had certainly needed such an escape.

Her fingers could still feel the grooves of the book's title, her hands the heaviness of its spine. She had opened it, and . . . and . . .

The thought that came to her next made her suddenly sit up in the unfamiliar bed. She didn't dare say it aloud, to herself or anyone else, for it seemed so bizarre. All the same . . .

Posy looked to the windowsill, intending to question the owl, but he was gone. A young maid in a simple gray gown approached Posy's bed and began to straighten the covers in a fidgeting way, as if she didn't know what was expected of her. The girl wouldn't look into Posy's face, even when Posy asked her for her name.

"Olena," the girl said, keeping her chin down and her eyes on her clasped hands.

"Olena," said Posy, thoughts of her own soft-spoken sister making her voice gentle, "I think you must know that I am not the princess, whoever she is, don't you?"

Olena's gaze shot up at once and her frightened eyes looked straight into Posy's. "Yes! That is to say . . . no! Oh, Princess! Please don't ask me such things!" And the girl flew from the room as if she were escaping something horrible.

Think, Posy said to herself. *Think hard. Where are you? How in the world did you get here? What were you doing last? Shouting at Mom and Dad—telling them to shut up, telling them I hated them. Yes, I remember that much. Then, at the library . . . finding the book, yes . . . taking it . . . feeling so strange . . . Opening the book . . . But that means . . .* Posy's mind swam and spun within her head. What *did* it mean?

"You are within the book, yes."

Posy started and turned toward the sound of the voice. The owl had returned and was sitting on the windowsill as if he had never gone, his soft gray and white feathers gleaming.

"In case you were wondering, which of course you have to be, you are within the book. That is really all I am at liberty to tell you for now, for things are a bit complicated within the Kingdom at present. Well, *very* complicated, in fact. I might tell you more at another time, but I don't know when. It can't be now. We need more privacy and I need more information. You will have to be patient, Princess."

"But why are you calling me Princess?" burst out Posy. "You must know I am no princess, and certainly not the daughter of any king and queen. I don't think you realize where I actually come from . . . It's nowhere like this!"

"Oh, of course it's nothing like this," the owl scoffed, ruffling his chest feathers. "No world is like this one. We are characters living within the Plot. And now you are one of us. But I can say no more—not now! I will find you when the time is right. In the meantime, *Princess*, I suggest you go along with whatever happens. It might be much less than pleasant if you decided to start talking and asking questions. No one asks questions here. You must follow the Plot. The king will have it no other way." The owl made ready to fly out the window once again. As he turned, his head swiveled around toward Posy and he said, "I am Falak, the king's chief adviser, if you have need of me. But you won't, because there is nothing else to say now." And he spread his great wide wings and dived off the windowsill and out of sight.

The thought slowly came upon Posy that perhaps it was no bad thing to be believed a princess. In fact, the more she thought of it, the more she liked the idea. How many times had she wished for just such a thing, as she sat curled on her bed enwrapped in a book?

As she lay on the enormous, soft bed underneath a silken coverlet, she began to feel very comfortable. Her fear and ignorance as to the way she had come to be I this strange place began to matter less and less. The owl had told her to play along, and she was only too willing if that meant living as a princess and forgetting the worries of her other life, which already seemed so far away. She determined that she would enjoy this adventure, even if it turned out to be a dream after all.

One thing worried her as she began turning things over in her mind. If this was a book, and it was full of characters, where had the *true* princess gone? And what if she came back and found Posy had taken her place?

About the Author

Ashlee Willis lives in the heart of Missouri with her husband, young son, and simply way too many cats. While most of her days are balanced between writing, reading and homeschooling, she also loves to crochet, play the piano, and spend time outdoors in God's creation.

Visit her author blog at http://ashleewillisauthor.wordpress.com
TWITTER: @BookishAshlee
FACEBOOK: AshleeWillisAuthor

www.ingramcontent.com/pod-product-compliance
Lightning Source LLC
Chambersburg PA
CBHW020542130626
46552CB00007B/2718